About

Adam Dickson is a novelist and screenwriter. His novels are *The Butterfly Collector* (2012), *Drowning by Numbers* (2014), *Billy Riley* (2020) and *Indigo Blue* (2022). He has also co-written three non-fiction books in the sports genre, and a book on mental health, *Surfing the Edge: a survivor's guide to bipolar disorder*.

His screenplays include adaptations of both novels, and a pilot for TV. In February 2020, he appeared as an expert in the CBS Reality crime series *Murder by the Sea*. The episode titled *Neville Heath, the Lady Killer* documents the real-life case of ex-RAF pilot Neville Heath, who was hanged at Pentonville Prison in 1946.

www.adamdickson.co.uk

A
Waltz
Through The
Dark Wood

by
Adam Dickson

Castra publishing

To Patrick
Best Wishes
[signature]

A Waltz Through The Dark Wood
Copyright ©2023 Adam Dickson

A special thanks to Alex Dickson for cover design and artwork.

ISBN: 978-1-7393207-0-6

Contents

The Girl

She was late – of course. What did he expect? Irritation gave way to relief, gratitude even, the way he always felt whenever he saw her. She took the seat opposite his, and eased herself down, flashing him a tight smile. With her hair tied back and sunglasses over her eyes, she had a vaguely mysterious look; something else she'd done just to confuse him.

'Sorry I'm late,' she said. 'I had to call in to work and pick up the keys for tomorrow.'

Mention of her workplace always threw him. Images of predatory men in suits all vying for her attention. She probably had her favourites among them too – a flash of eye contact along the computer banks to break up the boredom. The hint of seduction never far away.

She frowned at him. 'What's the matter?'

'I was just wondering where I came on your list of priorities. I've been sat here for three hours amusing myself waiting for you.'

'I said I was sorry, didn't I?' She sat back, deflated. Her churlishness suited her too, like the sunglasses and the swept back hair. All those subtle and not-so subtle shifts in attitude that conveyed a different meaning. One more facet of her that he couldn't work out. The ceaseless self-interest that informed all her decisions, an art form in itself. All those quirky aspects of her personality that somehow made her even more desirable.

'You want a coffee?' he said.

'I'm fine.'

'What's up?'

'Nothing. I'm just ... tired, that's all.'

Pedestrians passed by along the precinct, oblivious to the little drama acted out at their café table. He sensed something else, some private thought she might be trying to hide. The way she gazed off along the concourse, lost in thought. Already her act had slipped a little. He saw her as she really was, plagued by uncertainty and indecision like everyone else. Her chronic forgetfulness drove him crazy; the time she lost her new phone a couple of days after she'd got it, and then tried to blame him. Because of this he'd developed a mantra for whenever they left a restaurant or bar. 'Have you got your car keys, your purse, your handbag?' One more trait that made her who she was, which, aside from being frustrating, also amused him and endeared her to him at the same time.

Leaning forward, elbows on the table, he drank in the essence of her, the part of her that was always so elusive. She still wore the necklace he'd bought her that cost £450 – more than he'd spent on anyone before, even his ex-wife and children, who in the early stages of his career often went without. The fact she hadn't lost it was a minor miracle in itself.

'So what is it, then?' he said. 'Problems at work?'

'No?'

'I just thought you might've fallen out with someone. You've got that look on your face.'

She stared back at him. 'Do you want me to go?'

Her response caused him a stab of anxiety. She was clearly working her way around to telling him something he didn't want to hear, and he in turn had to prepare himself for whatever it might be.

The young Lithuanian waitress moved expertly among the tables with a tray of drinks. Apparently she had a boyfriend who worked in the kitchens. They went to great lengths to keep it quiet, but you could tell from the covert glances they gave each other that there was something going on. The unmistakeable spirit of romance that couldn't be hidden for long. The universal drive that gave life its energy and purpose, bringing the unlikeliest people together.

'Let's do something,' he said, keeping his tone deliberately light.

'Like what?'

'You're always saying we never go anywhere. We could go for a drive, take advantage of the weather.'

She shrugged, noncommittal.

Maybe it was the age difference, a worrying enough issue at the best of times. Twenty years was a fair sized gap, especially when you factored in things like musical differences and tastes in fashion. Most of her friends saw him as an oddity, someone they seemed to accept, who would always remain clueless about the world they inhabited. But even that didn't matter. Alone together they got on well. She was mischievous and affectionate, most of the time.

She turned a ring on her finger, and pursed her lips, chewing something over.

'I've been thinking,' she said. 'Everyone I know's doing something with their lives. What've *I* got to look forward to?'

'What's brought this on?'

She shrugged, turning the ring over and over. 'I just feel ... confused.'

'Because of me?' he said.

'Why's everything got to be about you all the time? There are other people in this world.'

Trying to work out her moods was the hard part. Every time he thought he'd got a handle on it, she'd make some remark, or do something out of character that would cause him to think again. But he had learned to read her to a point. When she was happy it transformed her whole being; she liked to tease him and pull silly faces, amusing him with impersonations of people she knew at work. When she was sad it was usually because of her job, or her moderately dysfunctional family, who were always a source of contention. He couldn't bear to think it might be something to do with him, that he'd pushed her to some unavoidable moment of reckoning.

Scooping out the froth from his cappuccino, he gazed out over the concourse. The Lithuanian waitress cleared a nearby table. She looked moderately happy, if such a condition was possible; always a smile for the customers, who sat in grateful anticipation as she brought out their food. As a writer, he liked to think he understood people's motivations. On the page, he could grapple with a whole range of emotional traumas, coaxing his characters through to a satisfactory resolution. They weren't perfect, but at least he knew why they did the things they did, and as a reward he got that godlike feeling of omniscience that came from being their creator. Real life wasn't as predictable. Things like divorce, bankruptcy and disillusion came along to interrupt the flow. Maybe that was another contributory factor. Life experience. All the things that'd happened to him over the course of several decades that increased his cynicism and ability to relate.

Bringing his focus back to the table, he observed the object of his ongoing fascination. She needed reassurance, that was the key. Women liked to feel they were being listened to, an area he'd neglected recently because of his work; the opportunities that'd opened up, taking him into new and exciting areas.

'How's your mum?' he said, searching for a neutral topic.

'Fine.'

'Does she still like me?'

Ignoring his attempt at humour, she stared at him behind the dark glasses. 'I don't know. Ask her yourself.'

They'd all got on well enough at first. Her mother didn't seem to have too much of a problem with the age difference, although he was closer in years to her than he was to her daughter. Sometimes, they'd even gone out as a threesome – enjoying reasonable success at the local pub quiz, in spite of his abysmal general knowledge, which contributed to their team coming last. Problems began when he went out to California to meet up with a production company. When he came back things were different between them, as if a conspiracy had started in his absence.

'How about we go away?' he said. 'Tenerife, maybe. You liked it there, didn't you?'

'I don't want to go anywhere,' she snapped, and averted her gaze. He tried to assess the damage, using all the things he'd learned about her in the two years they'd been together.

'OK, we'll stay here then. Doesn't bother me.'

The biggest problem was his own emotional investment. Maybe they should never have met. The more he saw of her, the greater his need for her attention. To disguise this potentially fatal weakness he assumed a kind of ongoing nonchalance, while secretly analysing his reactions to the things she said. Not a healthy way to conduct a relationship, but he couldn't seem to help himself.

He tried another tack, hoping to resurrect her sense of humour.

'How's life in the office? Have they replaced the cactus plant you murdered?'

'It wasn't my fault! No one told me they only had to be watered once every six weeks.'

'Hardly an excuse though, is it? Imagine how many times that's been used as a defence throughout history.'

Again, her ongoing silence deflected his attempt at humour. He tried to dismiss the increasing sense of foreboding that'd been creeping up on him since she'd joined him at the table.

'Talking of criminals I watched a documentary on Ted Bundy,' he said. 'When they finally caught him, he decided to conduct his own defence. You had to admire his nerve, really. Didn't do him much good in the end, though, he still got the electric chair.'

'Can we talk about something else?'

'Of course ... Why don't you ask me how my day's been, or is that not on the table for discussion?'

She checked her phone instead, distracted and clearly not in the mood. The 20-year age gap lay between them like a wilderness. People and events that'd come to symbolise his generation barely registered with hers. She liked pop groups he'd never heard of and crass TV reality shows. He liked history and works of art. And yet, she'd made the first move when they met, expertly manoeuvring herself next to him at a networking event, making it obvious to him *and* the woman he'd been talking to exactly what her intentions were. He'd been flattered, smitten perhaps. Then it all seemed to unfold naturally. The chemistry was there. But still she kept him waiting before she finally gave in.

Serial killers seemed to possess an uncanny ability to blend in and appear normal. Bundy was typical of the type, outwardly charming and inoffensive, harbouring a monster inside. The human component was missing. Inflicting pain and suffering didn't mean anything at all, except in terms of self-gratification. This apparent anomaly in human nature had become a major interest, a theme he ended up returning to in his writing, inspiring *The Velvet Glove,* one of his most successful screenplays to date, which first went out on HBO. She, on the other hand, didn't share his enthusiasm and found it all a bit disturbing. Perhaps that was why they'd bonded initially – opposites attract.

Gazing at her across the table, he pondered his dilemma. He longed to touch her, to feel connected to her physically. Each time they met was like the first, his desire for her setting traps he fell into regularly. She brought out the teenager in him, that surge of irrational optimism that kept him going for days on end.

In reality they were totally unsuited, of course – both in age and temperament. And yet he'd felt compelled to persist, chasing her using every angle he'd learned from his long and rudimentary study of women. Each advance he made became a sign of progress, victory even; an involuntary smile, or the sound of her laughter when he cracked an appallingly bad joke. Then, after they'd been together a while, came the hard part – finding ways to keep hold of her without compromising his self-esteem.

A young man in jeans and tee-shirt strolled past, and waved. She waved back, subdued but making eye contact.

'Who's that?' he said.

'Someone Melissa knows. She went out with him a couple of times.' Reading his dubious look, she sighed and shook her head.

'Don't start all that again. I'm really not in the mood.'

'Hey – I just asked who it was, that's all.'

'Yeah – and I know how your mind works. Just leave it.'

The vague threat from another male, always there in the background. Tribal conflicts that went back to the earliest primates, who feared the loss of ownership, status. Her boss, who was supposedly having an affair with his secretary; clearly the alpha male type, used to getting his own way. Strange how someone you'd never met could become a source of envy, competition even.

Talking about it made it worse. She always claimed to hate the man who ran the office like a despot, but this could've been a ruse to deflect attention from her real feelings. The conversations they had about him always went the same way.

'Why did his wife kick him out?'

'How should I know?'

'I thought he told you everything?'

'When did I say that?'

'Last week when I picked you up from work. You said he was thinking of giving you a bonus for being so understanding.'

'Oh, shut up – you're doing my fucking head in!'

Perhaps you could want someone too much – at least, more than they wanted you. A terrible price to pay for being so vulnerable and needy – the worse thing a man could be in the eyes of a woman. But again, the default setting: he just couldn't seem to help himself.

'OK, I give up,' he said. 'You're obviously not going to tell me what's going on. I'm just supposed to sit here all afternoon wondering what it is.'

She took her sunglasses off, and looked at him directly.

'I'm pregnant.'

The world stopped turning; the hum of voices around them faded; pedestrian figures passed by in a blur.

'I did a home test that was positive. The doctor confirmed it this morning.'

Any antagonism or tension between them gave way. He saw her in a different light, vulnerable and unsure, looking to him for support.

'How did it happen?'

'How do you think it happened?'

'But ... I thought you were on the pill?'

'I missed a few days ... Don't worry, I'm not planning on keeping it.'

'What do you mean?'

'Well I can't, can I? There'd be no point.'

'No point?'

She sighed, forced to explain the details to a child. 'Look – it was an accident. I never meant it to happen. It just makes sense to arrange a termination now, while it's at this stage.'

Termination. The word affixed itself to his brain like a limpet. It had a cold, clinical sound, as if she'd picked it up from some medical journal and was using it to justify her decision. Was it really as simple as that? One of the most momentous and life-changing events any couple could ever experience reduced to a simple expediency.

'I'll make the arrangements,' she said. 'You won't have to do anything.'

'So, I don't get a say in any of it?'

'What's there to say? What choice have I got?'

'You keep talking as if it's just you involved.'

'You're not the one who has to deal with it. It'll be me on my own, while you go on doing what you always do, obsessing about your job and going on about California.'

At least she'd included him in the dilemma in a roundabout way. The selfish man who'd had his fun and was now paying the consequences.

The thought crossed his mind that it might not be his. A simple test would prove or disprove paternity – the latter outcome absolving him of any responsibility. A wave of guilt followed. How could he even think such a thing? She wasn't like that. Sure, there'd been difficult periods between them, what with his work taking him away, and the problems that came up in any relationship. But essentially they were good together, enjoying a bond he hadn't experienced before. He'd never questioned her fidelity until now, and that was only in passing.

'Have you told your mum?' he said.

'Seriously?'

'I just thought – '

'She'd go mental, probably kick me out.'

A surge of wild and irrational hope arose within him. A child would bring them together, seal their union and make it more respectable.

'There is another option,' he said.

She stared at him, working out the implications.

'You're not serious?'

'Why not? I'm financially solvent – at the moment, anyway. You could always take maternity leave, if you're that bothered about your job.'

'And where would we all live?'

'We could look for somewhere. Rent an apartment or a house.'

She gave him a faint ironic smile, and slumped back in the seat, gazing off along the precinct. How beautiful she looked in that moment, her skin healthy and glowing in the sun, as if the first bloom of motherhood had attached itself to her already.

'What do you think?' he said.

'I just don't think it's realistic.'

'What – having a baby or living with me?'

'It's not funny.'

'OK ... How do you really feel? I mean, deep down? Do you want to get rid of it?'

She pursed her lips and sighed. 'I don't know. I can't think straight at the moment.'

The idea grew wings in his head, a soaring airborne vision of the three of them together. He'd have to break the news to his kids from his first marriage, of course, but this he would gladly do. And they'd be happy for him, glad he'd finally settled down.

'Look – I know it's a lot to think about,' he said.

'Don't put pressure on me, OK?'

'I'm not putting pressure on you ... Just don't go doing anything until we've talked it through. Will you promise me that much?'

She looked away again, the tangled lines of doubt and confusion unresolved. But already he was making plans for their future, ignoring the small voice at the back of his mind that suggested caution. The hopeless romantic in him, seeing the world in exotic colours – when it suited him. Perhaps this event, this unexpected happening, was just what he needed to sort himself out. No more drifting vaguely along, hoping life was going to change dramatically in his favour. A child would bring out the best in him – even if his track record in that department hadn't always been exemplary.

'Come on,' he said. 'Let's go for a walk.'

She frowned. 'Where?'

'The beach ... We can talk about it on the way there.'

They stood, drawing glances from the couple at a nearby table. He'd seen the look before, a quizzical assessment of their relationship status from the moral high ground. Was he her father, perhaps? Or one of those unprincipled types who took advantage of younger women?

He put an arm around her shoulder and gave her a lingering kiss on the cheek to dispel any ambiguity. They were an 'item'. Other people's opinion didn't matter. The love he felt for her was enough, in spite of all the factors weighed against them.

Strolling along the precinct together, it seemed that the sun shone especially for them. Life held promise. The gods smiled down, blessing their union. Soon he would be a father again, the chance to put right the mistakes he'd made with his own children. A kind of restructuring of the past. An atonement.

The Lover

Candice introduced us at the charity fundraiser she hosted at her beautiful country home. Right away I was taken with his looks – not conventional, but impressive in an overtly-male kind of way. He had the upper body of someone who worked out regularly – that inverted triangle you see in men's magazines, nicely defined but not too overstated. He had a younger man's energy, too, although he must've been in his mid to late-40s; he reminded me of one of those big cats, the way they prowl up and down looking for victims. The warning signs were there right from the beginning. He probably did this kind of thing all the time, hitting on vulnerable females, fully aware of the effect he had without even trying.

I found myself answering his questions with a defensive air, safe behind the barrier of my married status; the gold ring on my finger that might've put him off but probably wouldn't. His persistence was quite breath-taking, the way he leaned in to the conversation, focusing on poor little me, the object of his attention, to the exclusion of all else. Slowly, I began to be drawn in to his aura, the seductive smell of his aftershave – which he told me was Black

Absinthe, a name that for some reason seemed highly appropriate. And of course, his provocative body language that gave him such an allure. Comfortable, as the saying goes, in his own skin.

The conversation became a sort of game between us, where he was the hunter and I was the quarry. But far from being the innocent victim, waiting to be carried off to his lair, I knew exactly what he was trying to do and decided to play along with it. His attempts to schmooze me failed initially, although he kept chipping away with that disarming smile and movie star tone of voice, until it was all I could do to keep from leaping on him then and there.

'So you and Candice are friends, I take it?' he said, taking a sip of wine and eyeing me over the glass.

'Kind of. I know her through the charity she works for, but that's about it. I hardly know anyone here, so I'm sort of feeling my way in.' I took a sip from my own glass, my ring finger clearly displayed for full effect. He arched an eyebrow, but chose to ignore the gesture, firming his lips as he pondered his next move.

'So what do you do?' he said.

'In my spare time?'

He smiled, a twinkle in his eye to let me know he wasn't intimidated. 'I meant your job. I had you down as the executive type when I first saw you. You have that look.'

'Should I take that as a compliment?'

'Take it any way you like.'

Again, that casual sexual connotation barely disguised. And all the time he worked me with his eyes, in complete control of the game he was playing.

'I was actually in retail,' I said, steering the conversation back on track. 'I spent time in Japan and Hong Kong working for some of the big department stores.'

He nodded, the faintest hint of admiration perhaps.

'Sounds interesting.'

'Oh, it was. I loved it there – Japan in particular, it's such a vibrant place. At one point it was the world's fastest growing economy ... How about you? What line are you in?'

'I'm a trouble-shooter. I like to work on projects that take me out of my comfort zone.'

'Does that include chatting up strange women at fundraising events?'

'Sometimes.'

The stirrings of desire became a whirlpool. I tried to hang on to some vestige of self-control, but the same thought kept repeating over and over. What if I just gave in and let whatever was going to happen take its course? Already, the wicked voice in my head had subdued whatever was left of my conscience, and was happily leading the way. And yet, at the back of my mind was the unavoidable thought that what I was doing was wrong – and I hadn't actually done anything yet!

'I take it you're not married?' I said.

'I was, many moons ago. It didn't suit my disposition.'

'And what's that exactly?'

'I don't like to be tied down. I like to be free to move around, make my own decisions.'

A carefully laid trap I was falling into, but it was too late to back out now. We were hemmed in, alone by the unit with all the miniature glass figurines that sparkled like jewels beneath the fluorescent light. The hum of conversation filled in all around us; once or twice I noted an envious glance from a couple of the women, who must've wondered why he'd picked *me* to be the recipient of his charms.

Candice came over, positively glowing in her buttercup yellow dress. She touched his arm, casually intimate, the look she gave him lingering just a little too long; a shared complicity from some prior liaison perhaps.

'How are you two getting on?' Candice said.

'Fine – we were just discussing commitment, actually.' He smiled coyly at me to bring me into the equation. 'Marie was just telling me how she worked in Japan.'

I felt a little thrill that he'd remembered my name, that we were somehow bound together. Candice beamed back at us, as if this was just the thing she wanted to hear. Ever the matchmaker, expert at putting people together.

'Well look,' she said. 'I'm going to have to move on and talk to people, or I won't be doing my job. The presentation is due to start in about half an hour – if the speaker turns up. Let me know if there's anything you need, OK?'

When she'd gone, we resumed our stances, me with my wine glass held protectively close to my chest, him with his open body language, comfortable at all times and intent on his not-so secret mission. Alone with him again, I felt the irrational tug of desire. The combination of the wine and the intimacy of our narrow space in the now overcrowded kitchen made me long to be more daring. And like an expert in this static dance he teased it out of me, removing my inhibitions one by one.

'So – how do you know Candice?' I said, taking the initiative.

'She has me over every once in a while to look at her accounts.'

'You're an accountant?'

He laughed. 'Now you're insulting me to my face. As I said, I'm a sort of trouble-shooter. I see problems where others don't, then I'm paid ridiculous amounts of money to solve them.'

'That doesn't really tell me anything.'

'Ah – that's because I had to sign the Official Secrets Act before I took the job.'

'Like James Bond, you mean?'

'Could be.'

He had the most sensual mouth, that rolled the vowel sounds playfully and let them linger. I'm sure he must've worked on that tone of voice, too, the way it seemed to resonate in his chest, initiating a kind of hypnosis in his victims. Perhaps he really was a secret agent, and was having some fun at my expense.

'Look, it's really noisy in here,' he said, with a glance over his shoulder. 'Why don't we go outside?'

I made the mistake of agreeing, and as we stepped through the French doors onto the terrace, could've kicked myself for being so compliant. But there we were, removed from the main body of the party, relaxed in the tranquil evening heat.

Leaning in, one hand on the wall, he focussed on me again, closing off any avenue of escape.

'What else do you do?' he said. 'When you're not fundraising?'

'I have two young children. They take up most of my time.'

He nodded, as if in understanding, the unspoken insinuation that this revelation of mine should be no barrier at all. I felt the need to elaborate, not to be pigeonholed in any way. Yes, I was a wife and mother, but I had my own interests, my own mind.

'That's why I like being part of something positive,' I said, 'like the charity work. I can use my skills doing things for other people.'

'You have skills as well?'

'Yes – isn't that surprising?'

He did that thing with the raised eyebrow again, that seemed to accentuate the humour and magnify his intent at the same time. I felt like the heroine in a tacky romance novel whose fate is set. Unless someone intervened, I was going to be carried off to his castle and ravished, never to be seen again.

But the truth is, I wasn't doing much to discourage his advances. By now, I'd eased into a select performance of my own, giving him just enough eye contact, and angling my body towards his in an outwardly passive but deliberate way. All this was done without much prior thought, but as a natural response to the signals he was giving out – and the heady atmosphere that had developed between us.

One of Candice's helpers came out with a tray of wine glasses.

'Can I get you another drink?' he said.

'Why – do I look like I need one?'

He laughed, so natural and infectious that I laughed too.

Candice came out to join us, her deep Mediterranean tan contrasting with that yellow dress. She eyed us both with a devious, your-secret's-safe-with-me kind of look.

'Sorry I haven't been more attentive,' she said, and turned to me. 'Listen, Marie – I've offered to give Paul and Raymond a lift home. They did say they'd get a taxi, but I felt awful, especially as they've come all this way.'

I knew what was coming next, almost as if they'd planned it between them to ensnare me. Candice turned to my would-be seducer, and gave him a look of the sincerest appeal. 'Would you mind giving Marie a lift home? I don't think she's too far out of your way?'

So the deal was stuck, with me as the passive recipient, the observer in this ritualistic diversion. Perhaps they were in cohorts together, and Candice was the supplier of his victims, whom she would line up one after the other for him to knock off at leisure.

I tried to maintain my composure, to rationalise what had just happed. Why hadn't I insisted on making my own way home? Why had I allowed the situation to overwhelm me to such an extent? And yet, I knew why. The reason was becoming more and more obvious.

Candice left us to join another couple on the terrace. Right away, he turned to me with that faint smile in place, the certainty of his quarry now firmly in his sights.

'Whereabouts do you live?'

'Oh, it's not far from here. I can get a taxi, it's no problem.'

'And have Candice haul me over the coals for neglecting my duties? You wouldn't want to be responsible for that, would you?'

We left just after the presentation. Strolling out with him felt like the most natural thing in the world, as if we were a real couple going home to an apartment or a house in the country. The summer heat had stilled the evening air, making it warm and alluring, an invitation to the next stage, which by now had almost been written.

His car was parked out on the verge. Slipping into the passenger seat, I shut the door, and fastened the seatbelt. The interior was slick and clean, all black leather and polished chrome, a pervasive male scent that hinted at the corporate world he clearly came from. He eased himself in the driver side and shut the door, sealing us inside. Now I was in his world, and so far out of my depth I might easily drown.

All it took was one look. I threw my arms around him and drew him to me in a wild and luxurious embrace. Any notion of restraint or rational thinking left me then and there. The safe, domesticated life I'd lived prior to that moment had evaporated, gone in an instant.

He pulled back, his gaze caught by something outside. People were coming out of the house; they stopped to chat in the driveway, oblivious to our little spectacle.

'Take me somewhere,' I said, barely able to speak.

He drove wordlessly, both hands on the wheel. The doubts I'd entertained previously circled on the periphery, trying to get in. But I wouldn't let them. Nothing else existed except the furnace glow inside me, this primal need to be with him no matter what it took.

We parked in an isolated bay overlooking the sea. Fleetingly, I wondered how many times he'd been there before, and how many women he'd lured there the same way, but it no longer mattered.

He turned off the ignition, and the silence engulfed us, a tension that seemed to have drained all the air. I took a deep breath and closed my eyes, abandoning myself to the moment. His hands were all over me, expertly probing, manipulating. His mouth sought mine with the same urgency. I could taste the wine on his breath, the bittersweet scent of his aftershave, but most of all his exquisite maleness that overwhelmed and tormented me at the same time. I was lost, carried off to a place from which I never wanted to return.

Delicious pain. The sensation of being filled completely, beyond anything I'd experienced before. Wave upon wave of sublime electric impulses washed through my entire being. For some time I disappeared, my mind somehow detached from reality, carried away in an-ever expanding universe of pure bliss.

His back arched, his mouth open in a grimace of anticipation as he came inside me. Then it was all over, an act of completion that brought us both back to the physical plane. He sank back in the driver's seat, breathing heavily, his shirt open. Beyond the windscreen lay the darkened vista of the bay, a thin light out on the horizon. The aftermath. An uneasy peace that settled after the storm.

We rearranged our clothing, no longer together, but conspicuously apart.

'I'll take you home,' he said.

And that was it. No great speech to justify his actions, or make me feel less embarrassed at the situation we'd found ourselves in. Now all that was left were the practical considerations, the state of my clothing, my hair; the pack of tissues I usually carried that I'd somehow misplaced. Finally, an awkward acceptance of what'd just happened, and the need to extricate myself from it as soon as possible.

We drove in silence, the charm and the expert seduction left behind at the fundraising event, an act he no longer needed. I thought of Candice, with her knowing looks and subtle encouragement, as if the whole thing had been pre-planned. How would she see me now, my entire existence thrown into disarray because of that one casual introduction?

Now I had to go home and resume the staid and predictable life that'd taken me so long to construct, knowing it could never be the same again. And what of the man I'd married, the provider of my security, my children? The man who could never give me what I'd been given so consummately tonight? How could I ever look at him the same way?

I asked my accomplice to stop, a discreet distance from my house. I didn't want him to see where I lived, where my children slept unknowingly. Before I reached for the door, he put an arm out to stop me, a hesitant look on his face.

'Can I see you again?'

The uncertainty in his tone disappointed me. No longer the expert, the master of the game, he'd become needy and insecure.

'I don't think so.'

I stepped out of his car, acutely aware of the neighbours' vehicles parked at the roadside, and the lights from the adjoining houses. The first few steps I took away from him were empowering, the distance giving me the necessary space from which to recover. Adjusting my skirt as I went, I retouched my hair, hoping that the lipstick I'd reapplied in his pulldown mirror hadn't smudged in any way. But still I carried the unmistakeable essence of him inside me, and the memory of a lustful assignation that should never have happened.

Surprisingly, I felt no guilt. For one brief moment I'd shrugged off the demure, middle-class persona I'd been stuck with for so long and become someone else. I was, in a sense, free to embrace that other side of me. A sleeping tigress, unshackled from the chains of boredom and frustration that'd held me for so long. And in a strange way, he'd been the catalyst, conveniently put there at just the right time. Far from being the seducer, he had in many ways *been* seduced, then abandoned when his use was over.

My husband was asleep when I got in. I took a shower, and washed all the residue of that lustful assignation away, recalling the details as if they'd happened to someone else. Then I slipped into bed beside him and turned out the bedside light.

Paris

Arriving early, Colette noted the few customers with distaste. Old men smoking cigarettes and drinking ersatz coffee because they couldn't afford the cognac Cazal hid in his secret chamber. Their voices drifted over as she slipped off her coat, a discussion of food prices and the queues that seemed to get longer as time went on. Everyone suffered in one way or another, it just didn't do to advertise it, because you'd get no sympathy.

Henri came over to serve her, polishing the counter at the same time. They played a game where they pretended they weren't sleeping together, making conversation like normal people, and avoiding the little gestures that came naturally when they were alone. This little pretence amused Colette, until he ignored her to talk to one of the other girls. Then she wanted him more than ever, but this coupled with the desire to get back at him, just to get even.

He stopped polishing and eyed her casually, as if they were acquaintances, not intimate in any way.

'How are you today, Colette?'

'I'm well, thank you, Henri. A little tired, but that's to be expected, isn't it?'

He smiled coyly. 'Cazal was looking for you earlier. Have you upset him again?'

A ripple of alarm she tried not to show. She put on her haughty, dismissive voice. 'Cazal wants to be careful I don't throw in the job and go somewhere else.'

The old men had stopped talking, and were looking over. She eased her coat from her thigh to reveal a stockinged leg, anticipating their reaction. But cheap thrills such as this could be dangerous, even though it was part of her job; to dress provocatively was still a crime to some people, especially the older generation who considered themselves good French Pétainistes, the social reformers and morals guardians of the city. The eyes of the informers were everywhere, hooded and suspicious, ready to pronounce judgement on anyone found guilty of even minor infringements. But she couldn't help the little acts of 'rebellion' that helped ease the burden of daily living. Refusing to wear the drab clothing of ordinary housewives; preserving her feminine allure with elegant hats and makeup by Helena Rubinstein.

But there was a downside to all this causal extravagance. The diamond merchant, Hertz, had given her a dress from Shiaparelli, only days before he was arrested and deported. Because of this tragic outcome she could no longer wear such a beautiful gift, overwhelmed by the morbid association. Life in the city was characterised by similar episodes. People you'd known for years suddenly disappeared, and you didn't find out what happened to them until later.

Everyone tried to maintain the façade, the assumed air of normality that existed from the cafes to the boutiques. The city might be bound beneath the yoke of the oppressor, but it still had to go on day and night. There were titles to preserve and reputations to keep up. Shopkeepers still had to open for business and project a unified front, knowing full well that they could never keep up with the thriving black market. But the dark days wouldn't last forever. Even the most cynical could cling to that belief and find some hope in it.

'What're you doing later?' Henri said.

'Going home to bed – on my own preferably.'

'Well, if you need some company let me know. I could always walk you back – make sure you get there safely.'

'You're so kind, Henri. I don't know what I'd do without you.'

The old men had resumed their conversation, dismissive of her now that they'd seen a glimpse of her stockinged leg. She understood their attitude, even if she resented it sometimes; she was a threat to them – Colette, the purveyor of dreams to immature young men hoping for a tryst with an attractive girl. The soft and tempting flesh beneath her coat that they all came to see, a sight that caused men to behave in all manner of bizarre ways.

When she stepped out onto the stage under the house lights, she felt more alive than at any other time. The smoky atmosphere, the monochrome expressions of the men in the audience, all lent a hint of conspiracy, of collaboration, but in a positive sense. It gave her the illusion of power, when in all other areas she had none. She knew all the moves, having trained under Carlotta Zambelli and Gustave Ricaux. Her body was a symbol of expression, of inner freedom.

Henri drifted away to serve someone else. More customers wandered in, some she recognised, some she didn't. Young and old alike, they still had that obstinate Parisian disdain in their hearts, even if it was obscured by the need for survival. More than anyone, Colette knew the danger in showing too much verve or style, lest it be seen as a challenge by the ruling powers, the bureaucrats and committee members who decided how the city should be run. Those whose lofty positions had been subordinated to the new order, the day the German army marched into Paris and claimed ownership from that moment on.

Injustice and inequality abounded; weren't the wives and the mistresses of government ministers still wearing furs and expensive perfume when everyone else went without? But in spite of the attitude of resentment that abounded, many lives had been improved by the Occupation. You could see it in people's faces, the unmistakable glint of smugness, cheeks flushed with good living.

No one could deny that in many instances, life went on as before, with very little interference from the new hosts. The important thing was to blend in, to project a passive and harmless demeanour whilst going about your business. For the spies were everywhere, recording anomalies and signs of discord to be passed on to the authorities. Then everyone could pretend to be good French Pétainistes, and everything could go on as before.

The man she knew only as Jean-Louis came in, and spoke to Henri at the bar. The two remained in an intimate huddle, their voices deliberately muted. Colette tried not to look their way, but it was difficult. Jean-Louis inspired a mixture of emotions in her. He was often rude and offhand, treating her and the other girls with disdain, as if he was somehow above them. And yet he did have a noticeable presence; a member of the intellectual set that used to meet in the place Saint-Michel. But this in itself didn't justify his behaviour. Resenting him for his treatment of her, she was drawn to him at the same time, admiring his coarse good looks and noble mouth that rarely smiled, except perhaps in acknowledgement of someone else's misfortune.

Rumours went round that he was a member of the communist resistance group, Francs-Tireurs et Partisans. And now he would expect certain things from her that she was unwilling to give. Things that would have grave repercussions and put her own life in danger.

Without any invitation, he came over to sit beside her, removing his hat, and sweeping back his fine brilliantined hair with long, slim fingers. He seemed to be in no hurry, and casually took a cigarette from his packet, observing her with insolent good humour.

'How are you, Colette?'

'I'm fine, thank you.'

He nodded agreeably. 'I saw you riding your bike by the river the other day, and thought to myself, there goes the girl from Maxim's, she must be in a hurry. Were you meeting someone?'

'Perhaps, I don't remember.'

She tried to maintain the same nonchalant front so as not to encourage him, but his close proximity made it hard not to give in.

He lit the cigarette, and inhaled with great deliberation.

'Do you like working here?' he said.

'Sometimes.'

'And what about Cazal, does he treat you right?'

A trick question, she was sure, and one she had to be cautious answering. 'He treats me the same as he treats all the girls. We are all the same to him.'

Jean-Louis gave a nod, and brushed cigarette ash from his trousers the way he might swat a fly. He glanced over the bar, taking in the old men and the recent arrivals.

'This place is always busy,' he said. 'If you came in off the street you'd think nothing was unusual. The lights, the music, the dancing. Everything goes on as before, don't you think?'

'We all have to live.'

A flicker of irritation from him, perhaps. His reaction to her tone, the slight challenge her response had provoked in him. He knew as well as she did, that no matter how it appeared, nothing was as it had been.

'How is your father?' he said.

The question threw her, delivered as it was with a token innocence.

'Why do you ask?'

'He's been successful, his business thrives. The war has clearly been good to him.'

'My father has suffered like everybody else.'

Jean-Louis seemed to enjoy her response, the undercurrent of anger she couldn't quite conceal. The glint of amusement in his eyes only served to make him appear more intimidating, as if everything she said could be taken the wrong way and used against her. He reminded her of the Gestapo agents who came in sometimes asking questions. Perhaps he'd adopted their techniques and mannerisms, in order to elicit more information.

The old men got up to leave, easing their weary frames from the chairs. They left a collection of coffee cups and a full ashtray behind as a record of their visit. The club had changed since Colette had started as a naïve seventeen-year-old. The previous owner's wife had been accused of procuring girls for German officers. Someone had complained, and the rooms upstairs had been raided by the gendarmes. But the trade went on uninterrupted elsewhere, just as it always had done before the Occupation. When Cazal took over, the place had come to life again, as if he'd waved a wand and conjured up the glitter and the stardust that covered the stage floor.

'Do you follow what's happening in the rest of the world?' Jean-Louis said.

'In what way?'

'Have you heard, for instance, that the Allies have taken Caen, that Paris could soon be liberated?'

'Isn't it dangerous to talk like that?'

'It's even more dangerous to ignore the truth.'

He had an answer for everything, an air of superiority that seemed to hold everyone in contempt. Anyone would think the burden of occupation had fallen on him alone, and that Colette had somehow escaped all the indignities that went with it. The restrictions, the curfews. Paris had become a captive state, her citizens contained within its borders. The new occupiers had even brought the clocks forward to match the time in Berlin. Then other impositions to test people further; the introduction of the *Service du Travail Obligatoire*, where thousands of Frenchmen were deported to serve as workers in Germany.

'You don't say much, Colette?' Jean-Louis watched for her response, feigning disappointment. 'Is it my company you don't like?'

'I'm tired, I didn't sleep much last night.'

'And soon that will be the case for a great many people in this city. Those whose conscience is disturbed by the things they've done.'

She stared at him in alarm. 'What do you mean?'

'Do you know what it means to be a *résistante*? To risk your life every minute of the day?'

'I know what it – '

'A line has been drawn, like this ...' He traced an imaginary line on the counter with his finger. 'And everyone, without exception, will find themselves on one side or the other.'

He made a show of putting out the cigarette, taking his time.

'We need information. Troop movements. The transportation of arms and ammunition.'

'How could I possibly know such things?'

He smiled without humour. 'Don't be clever with me, Colette. I know the kind of things that go on here.'

She froze, hardly daring to look at him. His comment aroused in her a myriad fears and speculations. On the one hand, the allure of the club, and Cazal's patronisation, the smoke-filled nights and the illustrious patrons, who were most generous in their admiration of her and the other girls. Then there was the shadowland they all lived in – the restrictions and the shootings, the whispers of betrayal and collaboration that enfolded them all in a sinister web.

Jean-Louis watched her, with the quiet understanding that made him so unsettling.

'I know what you're thinking,' he said. 'You have a good life here in Paris, and you don't want anything to disrupt it. But things are about to change. Free French parachutists have landed in Morbihan. Sabotage units have been deployed. Those of us still here in the city are expected to do what we can.'

'I gave you information about Marie-Claude, didn't I?' she said. 'Told you where they'd taken her. Did I not put myself at risk?'

He nodded, lazily, humouring her, and she hated and feared him at the same time. The incident with Marie-Claude had unnerved her completely, especially given the suddenness with which it had happened. Arrested on the Rue Bonaparte for having false papers, Marie-Claude was taken to the SD headquarters in the Avenue Foch and interrogated. This was all Colette had been able to find out, but she'd passed the information on through the relevant channels. She felt bad for Marie-Claude. Not exactly friends, they had, however, worked together at the club, and shared the same secrets, the same collective sense of responsibility.

Now a far greater fear. It was rumoured that certain partisan groups had already begun compiling lists of known collaborators, in anticipation of liberation by the Allies. Jean-Louis was one of those men of which not much was known; he was an observer, quietly filing away all the things he saw to be used at the trials that would surely follow. Henri claimed he belonged to one of the underground cells that operated in and around Paris, where life expectancy and the possibility of capture was often a matter of weeks. But Henri claimed to know many things, and she didn't always believe him. In the atmosphere of fear and suspicion that persisted, it was better to say nothing, to know nothing, and above all to make sure you did nothing to alert the authorities.

Jean-Louis gave her a measured sidelong look, as if he knew what she was thinking.

'Who will you dance for tonight, Colette?'

Tired of his silly dramas, she drank her coffee, and watched the entrance. Hopefully, Sabine or Renée might come in and rescue her.

'I will dance for Paris,' she said. 'And for the liberation.'

Then a welcome glimpse of Cazal out in the foyer. She grabbed her bag from the counter.

'I have to go,' she said.

Jean-Louis watched her take off with that same sly amusement.

'Remember what I said,' he called out. 'A line has been drawn ... For you. For everyone!'

Climbing the stairs to Cazal's office, she went over his words, his suggestion that she might help with the resistance efforts in some way. His comments about her father, implying that he too had somehow betrayed the cause due to the increased productivity of his business, when so many others had to go without. Ever since the rumours had started that the Allies were closing in, the question of complicity had arisen more and more; the hard times of struggle and privation might soon be over, leaving in its place a different kind of war, one waged by those seeking vengeance against their own countrymen. Traitors everywhere, turncoats of the worst kind.

Cazal was standing by the window looking out over the rooftops when she went in. He rubbed his fat chin, as if vexed by some unidentified problem; the other hand was tucked into his waistcoat pocket. Right away she felt sorry for him, and a little guilty too, as if the source of his concern might be her responsibility.

'You wanted to see me?' she said.

He turned from the window, reminded she was there.

'Please, have a seat,' he said.

She sat the other side of his desk, and waited. He remained standing, in no great hurry to disclose whatever it was that was bothering him.

'Have I been good to you, Colette?'

'Yes, of course.'

'I've treated you with courtesy – in your estimation?'

'Is something wrong?'

He smiled sadly, a gesture that seemed to encompass the past and all its memories. She wanted to reassure him, to remind him that he was the best manager she'd ever had, but it seemed wiser to just listen.

'And the other girls?' he said. 'Sabine and Renée. What do they say about me?'

'They say the same.'

He observed her, nodding his head, but his gaze drifted again to the window. Maybe something had happened, she thought. A crisis of some sort that threatened the club.

With great effort, he turned back to her and straightened up, perhaps remembering his status at last. The Cazal they all knew and loved, whose flamboyance and flair for drama had made the place what it was. Even with the sandbags piled up outside, and all the statues removed, it still retained some of its old allure, and *he* had been the instigator.

Again, he sighed, a gesture that seemed to visibly diminish his bulk. He fixed his gaze upon Colette, eyes black as olives, misty with sorrow and regret.

'I'm leaving,' he said.

'Leaving?'

'We face a time of great uncertainty, Colette. It would be unwise for me to remain here any longer.'

'But where will you go?'

'I have friends in the south. And from there ...' His voice tailed off, the future an unknown prospect.

She didn't understand, confused by his demeanour, his tone. 'But what about the club? The girls?'

'I've asked Lecompte to take over. He knows the business inside out.'

The shock of such a departure. Cazal, who'd been there almost as long as Colette, with his little office on the top floor, reeking of cigar smoke and cheap brandy. He gave no reason for his decision, only the cloak of gloom which'd descended on him, leaving him bereft and unusually quiet.

He turned to the window again, as if the grey rooftops of the city contained the answer. 'The war will soon be over,' he said. 'Paris will be returned to its former glory. We must each make our own preparations for such an event.'

Jean-Louis' had made the same bold assumption, but with a distinct note of triumph, defiance even. In Cazal there was only resignation.

'If what you say is true,' she said, 'why don't you stay? What would we do without you?'

He remained quiet for some time. So intense was his rumination he seemed to have forgotten she was there.

'There are certain things we've all had to do in order to keep this place open,' he said finally. 'Certain *rules* we've had to obey. But my loyalty was always to you – to the girls and the club, the shows we put on.'

She knew the rules he was talking about. The priority that had to be given German officers, who always had the best seats in the house, the best cognac. The same rules that partitioned the city, making some areas *verboten*, restricting Jewish citizens to the last car on the Metro. Many French Jews had lost their businesses, their art collections, before being detained under the new laws. No one was safe. Even Sabine's father had to prove his ethnicity by producing baptismal papers for the police.

'I don't know what to say.' She glanced over the little office, a snapshot of somewhere familiar and reassuring, somewhere she may never see again. 'I feel so bad for everyone.'

He turned to her with a sad smile. 'I wanted to say goodbye to you personally, Colette, and to wish you every happiness. I only wish I could have done more for you, but ...' He took a handkerchief from his waistcoat pocket, and dabbed at his forehead – a result of the heat perhaps, rather than any display of emotion. 'One day we will all be free. And until that day comes ...'

The show that night reflected the mood of the city. The customers were a mixture of wealthy citizens and German officers stationed locally. As willing participants they became as one, united in their appreciation of the girls and the music. And how the dancers excelled themselves in their feathered boa costumes, darting out their stockinged legs in sync to the pounding rhythm. When it was time for Colette to come on, she felt the audience's embrace, as surely as if they'd wrapped their arms around her and hugged her to them. She danced for them as never before, as if her spirit had taken flight and soared high above the city.

Love and laughter – the only things that really mattered in life, that had somehow become the province of a select few – those who could afford to betray themselves with a smile, the odd flippant gesture to defy the authorities. Denied the right to flourish, the will found other ways to surface, creating new hopes and dreams from shattered lives and countless betrayals.

Finishing her dance, she looked out over the audience. There at the back, cigar between his teeth, little black eyes glinting in the shadows, was Cazal. She wondered what might become of him, and the thought made her unbearably sad. What might become of all of them, as the city's fortunes changed and the chaos of war was ended? He'd been good to them, it was true. Like a father in many respects, all through the girls' tantrums and the petty rivalries. Never once had he yelled at them or abused them in any way.

When the first act finished, she took a seat near the stage, and sipped from a glass of champagne, sent over by a German officer. Cazal had moved from his solitary place at the back, and was now talking to him. Bending down, one hand on the back of the chair, he nodded his head at something the officer had said. There was an intimacy about them, as if they'd known each other some time and enjoyed each other's company.

Cazal looked up, his gaze meeting Colette's across the smoke-filled room. And in that moment she understood why he had to leave. The truth was revealed to her in this mental snapshot of the two of them, Cazal and the German officer, framed in her mind as clearly as one of the portraits that hung in the foyer. Cazal's obsequious gaze and complicit manner, somehow enhanced by the officer's smug complacency. The uniform of the oppressor, that gave him an indisputable authority.

She understood her own guilt also. Years of living under the current regime and pretending everything was okay, when it was really a façade. All the people in the audience, the dancers on the stage. She saw them as they really were, playing a part, doing whatever they needed to do to survive.

Sabine came over, and sat with her. She looked over the officers and the regulars at the tables with the eye of one who has first choice at a banquet.

'I've never seen the place so busy,' she said. 'Look at them all out there.'

'It's because *you're* here, Sabine. They can't get enough of you.'

Sabine frowned, and gave her a childish look of resentment. 'I don't like it when you make fun of me, Colette.'

Sabine was a little dull – not through any fault of her own. For this reason men were able to take advantage of her, persuading her of things that simply weren't true. Colette always felt responsible for her, the few years between them giving her a reluctant seniority.

'Where's Cazal?' Sabine said.

Colette looked towards the table where he'd been only moments earlier. The German officer was still there, smoking a cigar, looking relaxed, convivial.

Cazal had gone.

She turned to Sabine, overcome with a sudden desperate affection, that same sense of responsibility now doubly painful. But what would be the point of trying to explain anything to her? All Sabine saw were the officers, the aura of prestige and charm they possessed. The chance to be transported away from the grim reality of the city, to a place of romance and excitement.

'Do you have any plans, Sabine?'

'What – for later?'

'No, I meant when all this is over. When the troops have gone home and we're free once again.'

Now *Colette* was the stupid one. Sabine shook her head. 'You say the funniest things, Colette. I think you must've had too much champagne.'

Sometimes people refused to see things that were there out of laziness, or because it was simply too painful to dwell upon. This worked for a time until it was too late. Sabine would ignore all the warnings, unable to see an end to it all.

Colette finished her drink, and stood, giving Sabine a kiss on the cheek. Sabine looked at her with the same quizzical smile.

'Where are you going?'

'Home.'

'Did I do something to upset you?'

'No of course not ... Goodbye, Sabine.'

She collected her coat from the concierge, and headed for the door. No one tried to stop her or ask where she was going.

Outside, people were milling by the club's entrance. There was something different about them, in their manner and in the clothes they wore. Normally, the streets were fairly quiet at this time, with everyone following the strict curfew. Tonight, the mood was different, as it had been inside the club, the crowd quietly expectant as if waiting for something to happen.

Two German soldiers came towards her, rifles slung across their shoulders. They barely noticed her as they passed, lost in mid-conversation. Their accents grated, the language of the oppressor she'd never quite got used to. And yet there were two facets there, the one harsh and brutal, the other kind and forgiving. Painful memories of a brief but passionate affair which had consumed her completely.

Long after the soldiers had gone, she could still recall their faces, the tedium of their daily patrols giving them a detached and insular appearance. They were only young, probably grateful not to have been sent to the Russian Front like so many of their countrymen. But they were still the enemy, especially to men like Jean-Louis. And now he'd infected her with his cynicism, as if doing nothing was a crime every bit as serious as collaboration.

Climbing the stairs to her room, she felt light-headed, almost nauseous as if she'd drunk too much on an empty stomach. The boards creaked as she made her way along the corridor to her room. Mrs Garnier would probably be on the other side, one ear to the door, ready to pass on the details of her movements to anyone who cared to listen.

Once inside, she packed a case, folding a few clothes and undergarments. Nothing much to miss about the room except the faded wallpaper and the skylight window where the pigeons held regular conferences. But she would miss the club and all the colourful people – especially Cazal, who in the end had reached out to her with a genuine concern, his melancholic mood almost palpable.

Searching through a drawer, she found the brooch that Werner had given her. She held it in the palm of her hand, and gazed at it with a strange longing. It felt so innocent, the gift from someone so far from home, someone who'd loved her and wanted to show his appreciation for all the pleasure she'd given him. And yet to even think of such a thing was dangerous. Better to forget that it had happened, the remnant of a dream dissolved in bitter reality.

She packed the brooch alongside the few books and papers she'd included. No one need know. Werner had gone back to Germany, recalled to the original unit he'd served in before he was sent to Paris. And they'd been discreet, at her insistence, using his apartment on the Rue de Crimée, only using her room occasionally for convenience. The only people who did know were those who'd indulged in similar illicit affairs themselves – girls like Sabine and Renée, who for one brief moment found themselves in a different world, able to enjoy all the privileges and benefits denied everyone else. But for all their naivety, they must've understood the retribution such actions could bring – especially now that the course of the war was changing. Colette only had to recall Jean-Louis' brooding face at the bar. *A line has been drawn ... For you. For everyone.*

Leaving with her case, she took the backstreets, where even the soldiers didn't patrol; her papers were in order and would guarantee her safe passage to the outskirts of the city. From there she could make contact with her uncle, and arrange to stay with him for a while, awaiting news of the Allied invasion. The familiar apartment buildings seemed party to her escape, enveloping her in a protective shield. Perhaps one day when it was all over she would come back, and resume her dancing career at the club. Until such time it was best to leave, to escape the vengeful nature of men like Jean-Louis, who might hold her accountable for the things that had happened. For the single, unpardonable crime of falling in love.

A roadblock appeared up ahead, a German truck parked across the intersection. A soldier leaned against the tailgate, smoking a cigarette. He saw her and straightened up, something to relieve the boredom, no doubt. She fished in her bag for her papers, assuming her little act without thinking. The Maquis used girls for the same reason, for theirs was a persuasive and beguiling charm that disarmed the enemy and made him vulnerable.

Approaching, Colette prepared her little speech, her smile in place. The soldier smiled back, barely in his twenties, the collar of his uniform unbuttoned. All they wanted was for the girls to be nice to them, so they too could forget the war and all its iniquities. Then one day when it was all over, they could go home and rebuild their lives. Paris would be left as she was before, haughty and indifferent, ready to trade once again in the currency of love and laughter.

'Papers?' the soldier said.

Colette handed them over, aware of a Swastika flag draped high up from a tenement window. One more vain attempt to subdue the city and its people.

The soldier handed her papers back, and gave her a diffident smile. She thanked him, and walked away, into the shadowy streets of Paris, and an uncertain freedom.

Hansel and Gretel

There once was an old woodcutter who lived on the edge of a large forest with his second wife and two children. They managed well, within the constraints of his slender budget, and he in turn treated them with kindness, only taking ale on a Friday night and always returning before sunup the next morning

Sadly, however, the children's stepmother was of a different ilk. Rather than share her husband's affection for the children, or the contents of the dining table provided by him, she made sure they had only crumbs, and insisted they ate in the kitchen out of the way. Being somewhat stern and vindictive by nature, she ruled the household with an iron grip.

One night, lying in her soft, downy bed after a bout of vigorous lovemaking, she conceived of a plot to rid herself once and for all of the troublesome pair. Turning to her husband, the passive recipient of her dubious charms, she outlined her plan, reminding him of all the things she'd done for him, and how little he'd done for her in return.

'Winter will soon be coming,' she said in summary, 'and we

shall have two hungry mouths to feed in addition to our own. We can no longer afford to keep them here. You must take them into the forest and leave them there.'

'But they are my children,' the woodcutter protested. 'I have a duty to care and protect them.'

'Then it is I who will go instead.'

The stepmother's deviousness paid off. Overcome with fear at the thought of losing her, the woodcutter hesitated. Being a man of principle, brought up on the strict religious values of his Lutheran parents, he couldn't give in to his wife's demands without a fight.

"What you're asking me to do is tantamount to murder,' he said. 'I will not do it.'

'As you wish. I shall pack my case and leave this very minute!'

The woodcutter pondered his dilemma. Abandoning the children would in fact bring certain benefits, it was true. There would be more food for him and his wife, and he would not have to toil quite as hard to provide sustenance. Plus, they would have more time to be intimate, and he would get to sample the goods, which were often withheld due to the close proximity of the children.

This, and other reasons, brought him to an uneasy, but nonetheless compelling decision.

'I will agree on two conditions,' he said.

Sensing victory, the children's stepmother eyed the woodcutter with barely contained glee.

'And what are they?' she said.

'That you frequent the marital bed as often as I request, and stop beating me for no good reason.'

Being a woman of some discernment, the stepmother saw room for future negotiation. A compromise would reduce her bedroom duties to an acceptable minimum, giving her more time for beauty products and reality TV.

'Very well then,' she said. 'But you must act swiftly and without delay.'

The next morning, with a heavy heart, the woodcutter took his brood deep into the forest. They whined and complained, as children do, when expected to walk long distances without recourse to entertainment, but to no avail. Their father's mind was set. And the further they wandered beneath the dark canopy of tall trees, the more fearful they became.

Finally, their father stopped and turned to them with tears in his eyes.

'Goodbye, children,' he said. 'I must leave you here.'

'But father, please!' Gretel clung to his arm, imploring him. 'You cannot leave us here at the mercy of fate, for we shall surely die and be eaten by wolves.'

'Don't worry,' he said. 'I'll find you some wood to make a fire, then I'll be back.'

And with a deviousness born of desperation, he was gone, making his way through the forest from whence he came.

Now, stranded and truly alone, the children hugged each other and wept bitterly at their fate. And all around, the gnarled and twisted limbs of the trees seemed to enclose them in a sinister embrace.

'Whatever shall we do?' cried Gretel, drying her tears with the back of her hand. 'We shall never live to see Christmas presents, or play on a bouncy castle again.'

'Don't worry,' Hansel said. 'When our dear father brought us here, I took the precaution of leaving a trail of white pebbles behind to show us the way. All we need do is follow them and we'll be out in no time.'

Gretel wept with joy at this unlikely development and hugged Hansel even harder. 'Oh, Hansel,' she said. 'You're so enterprising. It's one of those qualities I've always admired in you.'

'Well,' he said, with a humble shrug. 'Desperate times and all that ... Now let's push on and find the way back before it gets too dark.'

And so the intrepid pair made their way back through the forest, picking up the trail Hansel had left behind. When night fell they were able to navigate by the light of the moon that shone on the surface of the pebbles through the trees.

Arriving back near their home in the early hours, they stopped to catch their breath. Lights from the windows cast the woodcutter's cottage in a fireside glow, making the interior look warm and inviting. And yet they both understood the implications of venturing any nearer.

Gretel shivered with grim foreboding. 'What about our stepmother? Won't she be angry at our return?'

'Don't worry about her. We have certain inalienable rights which would be upheld in any court of law.'

But Gretel's misgivings were justified. The next morning, the stepmother discovered their return and went ballistic, shutting herself in her room and refusing to come out until they were gone from sight. The poor beleaguered woodcutter tried to reason with her, claiming it was an unforeseen accident that they'd come back, and therefore not his fault. But his wife refused to listen, incensed that her plan had been foiled.

'You've let me down once again,' she said. 'Now we'll have to put up with the pair of them indefinitely, a burden on our pitiful resources.'

The woodcutter tried to resolve things with whispered endorsements of his feelings for her, and kisses to her slender neck. But she shut up shop, and turned to him with a vindictive gleam in her eye.

'Don't think you'll get round me like that. There'll be no more horseplay in this house until those kids are banished forever!'

Being a rather weak-minded fellow with simple needs, the woodcutter pondered this intractable problem and came to a desperate conclusion.

'OK,' he said. 'Tomorrow, I will take them into the forest again. And this time I'll make sure they never come back.'

Intrigued by his forthright manner and solemn tone, his wife stared hard at him.

'You mean? ...'

The woodcutter's silence confirmed her suspicions, and a murderous complicity set in between them. And thus began a plot of nefarious designs, with the sole purpose of ridding the household of its surplus cargo.

The next day, as good as his word, the woodcutter again led his children into the forest, the onerous nature of his task heavy upon his brow. But unbeknown to him, Hansel had anticipated the ruse, and sprinkled breadcrumbs on the path behind them to point out the way. And when they reached a point deep in the forest that called for their parting, he felt certain that they could follow the trail and get back safely again.

Torn between loyalty to his wife and the love of his children, the woodcutter hesitated. In his backpack he carried an axe, which he'd agonised over using all the way along. But finally, faced with the reality of such a terrible prospect, he broke down and sobbed wretchedly, bidding the children farewell.

'I'm so sorry,' he cried. 'I can only hope that one day you'll find it in your hearts to forgive me.'

And so, with the same vague promise to find wood for them to build a fire, the woodcutter hurried off and did not return.

Alone in the dark forest with no one to turn to, Gretel started to cry. Hansel hugged and tried to comfort her, but the night soon closed in, and with it a sense of desolation and loneliness such as they'd never experienced before. The shadows took on ominous shapes, the trees like sentinels, thick and impenetrable all around. A wolf howled in the distance, a rallying cry to its compatriots, who might be keen to take advantage.

But being an enterprising child, who'd read books on survival, Hansel unveiled his plan: the trail of breadcrumbs he'd left would highlight the way and they'd be back in no time. Gretel stopped crying, and felt a tiny thread of hope, again putting her faith in her brother's resourcefulness. Yes, they would pick up the trail and soon be home, where they could initiate legal proceedings against their stepmother.

Alas, Hansel hadn't reckoned on a simple fact of nature. The birds of the forest had swooped down and eaten the breadcrumbs up. His optimism turned to despair, and he found himself in the grip of a profound depression.

'What are we going to do now?' Gretel cried. But alas, Hansel had no answer. They were children after all, limited in their understanding of life and its grim realities. Now they were at the mercy of a perverse universe that cared little for either one of them.

And so together they stumbled on through the darkness, the crack of twigs and the rustle of fallen leaves amplified beneath their feet. The eyes of the forest's wild inhabitants watched them in silent appraisal. It seemed that this was to be their fate, to be devoured by wild animals, their bones left as a warning.

At last, tired and hungry, they came to a clearing, within which sat the most charming looking cottage, bathed in the light of the moon. A thin column of smoke rose from its chimney.

'Look,' said Gretel. 'There must be someone inside. We're saved!'

But Hansel stressed caution; he'd watched too many episodes of *CSI* to go charging in without first making a reconnoitre. So they crept up on the strange looking abode, and had a closer look.

What they discovered made them gasp in astonishment. The exterior seemed to be constructed entirely of confectionary! Huge chunks of marzipan formed lintels over the windows; thick slabs of shortbread formed the walls. A layer of pink icing coated the roof, the eaves of which were made of fudge.

Breaking off a large chunk of dairy milk chocolate from the eaves, Gretel took a tentative bite. She murmured with pleasure.

'Hansel!' she cried. 'This is truly amazing!'

'Careful,' he replied with a twinkle. 'Remember what happened when you ate that apple.'

Ignoring his obscure biblical reference, she sank her teeth into the chocolate, and her eyes lit up with a rapturous delight. Encouraged by her example, Hansel snapped off a piece of marshmallow topped with little edible stars. Together, they absorbed the succulent fare, unaware that the door to the cottage had opened, and they were being observed.

There in the doorway stood a wizened old woman. She wore an apron fastened at the waist, and had clogs on her feet. Her hooded eyes and long, hooked beak came straight from central casting.

'Well, well, well,' she said to herself. 'Look what providence has brought me. How exciting!'

Realising they weren't alone, the children stopped eating and froze. The old woman beckoned them over, so she could see them in a better light. With some trepidation, they approached, and stood nervously before her.

'My, how lithe and supple you are,' she said, reaching out to feel Hansel's arm. 'I expect you work out regularly, don't you?'

Unfamiliar with the terminology, Hansel looked confused. But the old woman was quick to capitalise on her good fortune, and opened the door wider to reveal a cosy interior, where a fire burned in the grate.

'You must be cold and tired,' she said. 'Come in and rest a while, and I'll find you something else to eat.'

And so began the next phase of the children's development, a saga of betrayal and neglect, and the abdication of parental responsibility. It highlighted the plight of children the world over, and the actions of certain unprincipled individuals who contribute to their suffering.

But like many seasoned predators, the old woman proved to be adept at manipulation, and did indeed make Hansel and Gretel feel welcome. However, as if often the case with such pathological types, she began to reveal aspects of her character which were at odds with the image she wished to portray. Coupled with the tendency to cackle to herself for no apparent reason, she had a fine line in sarcasm, which she used to especially good effect when reminding the children of her selfless hospitality.

Being somewhat less naïve than his sister, Hansel grew suspicious and confronted the old woman, demanding to know her real intentions. At this, she dropped her kindly façade and grew cold and mean, pointing a gnarled finger in his face.

'Now you listen to me, sonny,' she said. 'I've had just about enough of your whinging – and after all I've done for you. It's no wonder your father kicked you out.'

'What're you going to do to us?' Gretel said fearfully.

'I'm going to fatten you both up and eat you – that's what I'm going to do! And we'll start with you, young man.' She prodded Hansel in the chest, a wicked glint in her eye. For unbeknown to her hapless guests, eating children was her MO, a perverse cannibalistic streak that'd run in her family for several generations. And although Hansel felt intimidated by her outburst, he was reluctant to act due to long-ingrained protocol issues that dictated how the young should relate to the old.

And so, their diabolical host set to work with commendable vigour. To keep Hansel incapacitated while she carried out her plan, the old woman kept him imprisoned in a cage that hung suspended from the cellar ceiling. Over the next few days, she fed him stew and dumplings, and other tender morsels from her pantry until he could eat no more. All Gretel could do was watch, terrified of the old crone, who chuckled and muttered to herself as she went about her infernal business.

At last, satisfied that Hansel was as stuffed as a plump chicken, the old woman went to the oven door to check the heat. The roaring furnace inside almost singed her hair as she bent to assess its readiness.

'Oh yes!' she said to herself. 'Better than gas mark 7.'

The implications dawned on Gretel, who pictured her poor brother being roasted for the old woman's depraved appetites. And while he remained helpless in his cage, unable to help, Gretel felt compelled to speak out.

'Why are you doing this?' she cried.

Distracted from her labours, the old woman looked up, a mean glint in her eye.

'Why? Because I hate children like you and wish to rid the world of them, that's why; there's also their superior nutritional content, but that's another story.' Seeing Gretel's confusion, the old woman adjusted her position, adopting a more matronly approach. 'Now come over here and check the oven's hot enough. I can't quite see with my eyes.'

Dutifully, Gretel went over, and opened the heavy oven door. The heat leapt out at her, causing her to recoil. But aware of the old woman's intentions, she feigned ignorance, and called out behind her.

'I can't tell if it's hot enough. You'll have to see for yourself.'

Irritated, the old woman pushed her aside, and bent to inspect the fire.

Seized with an uncharacteristic compulsion, Gretel Leapt up, and with one almighty effort, pushed the old woman into the oven, and slammed the door!

Freed from his steel cage in the cellar, Hansel hugged Gretel, whose quick-thinking had save them both from a terrible fate.

'Come on,' he said. 'Let's ransack the place, then head for home.'

Gretel looked at him in consternation. 'But won't that exacerbate any charges made against us?'

'Don't worry about that,' Hansel said, reasserting his moral superiority. 'We acted in self-defence. There isn't a jury in the world that would convict after hearing what we've been through.'

And so, with backpacks stuffed with food and valuables taken from the cottage, the pair vacated the premises and began their search for home. Armed with a new resourcefulness gained from their dealings with the wicked world, they were both changed in subtle ways. Although still only children, they'd learned the age old dictum 'kill or be killed', an accompaniment to survival down through the ages.

Soon, they met a travelling tinker who took pity on them and promised to show them the way. With his help they were guided at last to the track at the edge of the forest that led ultimately to the woodcutter's dwelling. They were sad to see the tinker go, having enjoyed his company. He seemed a jolly fellow, who by his own admission had suffered a run of bad luck. After an encouraging start selling time shares in the Bavarian Alps, he'd been forced to retire after an avalanche buried the ski lodges under 15 feet of snow. Then, as if that wasn't bad enough, his wife left him for a shoe salesman, which severely impacted his self-esteem.

Hearing of the children's misfortune, he was quick to give advice.

'I know a good lawyer, if you need one,' he said. 'It's all about litigation these days. Even kids need a decent brief.' He handed Hansel a business card. 'Give me a call on that number. I'll be happy to set something up for you on a no win no fee basis.'

With a grateful farewell, they set off along the track, debating what they should do next. Still undecided about the tinker, Gretel sought Hansel's opinion.

'Funny little fellow, wasn't he?' she said. 'Do you think he was on the level?'

'He seemed decent enough. But you can't be too careful these days – as we found out.'

After some time, they came to a wide river, and there on the bank was a most incongruous sight. A frog arguing with a scorpion.

'What are they talking about?' Gretel said.

Hansel observed the curious spectacle, and shrugged. 'They seem to be haggling over something. But whatever it is, it won't end well for the frog.'

'Why?'

'Because they'll strike some kind of a deal, and the frog will come off worse, just to prove some obscure philosophical point.' Hansel gave his sister an affectionate hug. 'Come on, let's find a way to cross this river.'

As luck would have it, they found a little wooden boat tied to a jetty – left there deliberately by the production unit of a Disney epic. And off they went, with Hansel rowing energetically for the other side. Gretel beamed with admiration at her brother's ingenuity. She couldn't wait to get home and rearrange her doll's house, giving them all new directives. Life was promising again. There were balls to attend, like Cinderella, and boy bands to scream at whenever their tour came to the local theatre.

By nightfall, tired and hungry after their ordeal, they reached the woodcutter's cottage. There it was, nestling in the wood like a shrine to domesticity. The family home they'd shared for all these years with their beloved father.

Wary of making any sudden moves, they stood some way off and observed the dwelling through the trees.

'What should we do?' Gretel said.

'There's only one course left open to us. We must wait until father leaves for work, then go in and confront our stepmother.'

Gretel looked at him with grave concern. 'You mean? ...'

'There is no other way, Gretel. She's forced our hand.'

Duly, the following morning, the woodcutter left for work, with his backpack and axe. The children longed to run to him and share their joy at being released from the old woman's evil clutches. But restraint was called for, and a degree of planning as to the next move.

Once their father had gone, they crept around to the back door, knowing it would most likely be open. Hansel tiptoed inside, careful not to make a sound upon the flagstones. Gretel followed, peering anxiously for any signs of movement within.

Peering round the door that led to the living room, they drew in their breath. There by the fireplace, warming her hands, was their stepmother, the woman who'd abandoned them and brought such misfortune upon their heads.

Seeing them, she froze, a look of terminal shock on her face.

'What the devil are you doing here!' she said.

'We've come to reassert our rights,' Hansel said. 'And to ensure you get your come-uppance.'

'Get out!' she yelled, her eyes blazing like the coals in the hearth.

'It's you that must leave,' Gretel said. 'We will not put up with your tyranny a moment longer.'

Drawing herself up to her full height, the stepmother glared at them both.

'This is *my* house, and I will not leave it for anyone, least of all the likes of you.'

'We'll see about that!' Hansel said, and in one swift move, snatched his father's ceremonial axe from above the fireplace.

Reacting swiftly, the stepmother grabbed the copper skillet that stood by the fireplace, and turned to her assailant.

'What makes you think you've got the balls to take me on?' she sneered. 'I gave your father a damn good pasting and I'll gladly give you one!'

Like gladiators in the Roman arena they faced each other, looking for the right moment to strike. Gretel watched anxiously from the sidelines, too frightened to intervene.

In a bold move, the stepmother swung the copper skillet

at Hansel's head. Too quick for her, he stepped to one side, and parried the blow with the ceremonial axe. Around the living room they went, dislodging ornaments and scattering pieces of furniture in a deadly waltz.

Then, in a breath-taking moment of suspense, the stepmother tripped on the fireside rug, and fell face down at Hansel's feet.

Seized with a sudden frenzy, Gretel leapt up and yelled a partisan cry in Latin.

'*Habet, hoc habet*! Do it, Hansel! Finish her off!'

And before you could say 'Anne Boleyn', Hansel swung his father's ceremonial axe and took his stepmother's head clean off!

Exhausted from his efforts, he dropped onto the worn sofa, still covered with the blood spatter which would be used as evidence by forensics later. Gretel fetched him a restorative glass of lemonade, and sat beside him, pondering the enormity of what they'd done, and the unlikely fact that they were now both serial killers.

When the woodcutter returned home that evening, he was greeted by the sight of his estranged children, who ran to greet him.

'Papa!' Gretel cried, flinging her arms around him. 'We've come back to you!'

And what a homecoming it was, even amidst the blood-stained walls and the scene of carnage. The unfortunate stepmother's body parts were buried among the vegetables in the back garden in a short and moving ceremony. The woodcutter consoled himself with the likelihood that there would be other offers, especially with the insurance money that would come in, plus the fact that he was still relatively good looking.

'There,' Hansel said to his dazed and still open-mouthed father. 'We've been reunited. You need never abandon us again.'

So the three sat down and ate a hearty meal in celebration, and in the tradition of all good fairy tales, lived happily ever after.

Footnote: Actually, they didn't. The trial of Hansel and Gretel lasted six months, generating a media frenzy and intense debate among the public at large. The Judge accepted the defence's claim that there were mitigating circumstances, but ruled that there was also a degree of premeditation – especially in the case of the stepmother. The jury found Hansel guilty of manslaughter due to diminished responsibility and sentenced him to five years youth custody. Gretel was given a conditional discharge, pending further psychiatric reports, and went to live with an aunt by the sea. She visited Hansel regularly, and brought him the books and papers he needed for his Law degree, as well as the chocolate buttons he'd since developed a craving for. She later wrote a best-selling book on their adventures, and advised on the film production that followed. Hansel was released after serving his sentence, and did not reoffend.

Sector 9

Looking out from his window on the third floor, Harris saw the boy on the bike again. For some reason, the sight instilled in him a strange and forlorn hope for the future. One day things would be different. All the trials and impositions people had to endure now would be a memory. Something in the boy's demeanour moved him; the way he gripped the handlebars and stared resolutely ahead, turning the pedals over and over with grim intent. The tyres left a slick on the asphalt that'd been baked in the sun, but the boy's face reflected only the nobility of his mission as he passed by on his way to the next intersection.

Perhaps he's visiting a sick relative, Harris thought, an ageing grandmother isolated in one of the tower blocks by the canal. The elderly were dying in their hundreds, refused medication or treatment unless they were on one of the select 'lists' stored on a government filing system. That which nature couldn't hasten naturally, the Department of Health could by mandate, issuing their latest edicts through the news channels, and all the major media outlets they now controlled. During the last case of civil unrest, the militia had been deployed, but the dissent had been short-lived. The ringleaders were rounded up and imprisoned, there to await a mock trial and the inevitable punishment. Harris had escaped, partly because of the few influential friends he still had. But for how long? The net was closing. Soon he'd be forced to make a decision, leave his single room in the tenement block and head for the border.

When the boy had gone, the tomblike silence set in. The windows in the block across the street looked glazed over, almost opaque in the afternoon sun; the radio aerial on the roof rose like a ship's mast, its tip pointing ever upward. A lone crow perched on the parapet, its oily black wings furled and sleek. It looked down on the neighbourhood like a sentry, observing the empty street for signs of movement.

Way off in the distance, the blast of a factory horn sounded the four o'clock changeover from one section of the workforce to another. With the closure of the main plant in Sector 5, the remaining workers had to fight for their positions, while the newly unemployed shuffled off to their homes with a miniscule payout. An aura of gloom had descended on the city, the boarded up shopfronts reflecting the citizens' plight. But with no organised resistance, the opposition was restricted to a few isolated demonstrations, which were soon contained by government forces. Harris himself had been instrumental in identifying and removing the most prolific troublemakers, adding names to a database that grew ever longer. How ironic, that he should now be a target himself, forced to abandon his former life of luxury for one of almost Spartan deprivation. They had his name, his face. It was only a matter of time before one of the snatch squads came calling.

At five o'clock, the first trickle of humanity appeared on the streets for their hour of exercise. Looking down on them, like the crow on the parapet, he felt a lofty indifference to their fate. The proles, faceless automatons, no longer able to call themselves a collective, but a string of individuals who'd given up the fight. They drifted listlessly along in their twos and threes, each given to a kind of morbid reflection, heads down, hands in the pockets of their threadbare jackets. Told what to do by the daily news bulletins, content to let the government propaganda machine do their thinking for them. To resist was to go underground, to join the disparate band of rebels who met in secret places and shared classified information leaked from equally secret sources. Posters in the city labelled them 'Recidivists', incorrigible backsliders intent on undermining the government by spreading lies and misinformation. To contain the problem the entire city was employed to identify and report them to the authorities. Take them off the streets before they brought down the entire system.

And yet, he too was one of them now, an outsider, a recidivist. The private schools and the country estate were a thing of the past. He belonged nowhere but here now – in this threadbare room with its single lightbulb and faded wallpaper. And yet a part of him still identified with the government department he'd given half his life to. Schooled in the arts of surveillance and infiltration, he spoke three languages, and had a charming and personable manner. He could win people over when he needed to, then, just as easily, have them rubbed out.

A woman in a faded shift dress filed past below him. He watched her go by, thinking how incongruous she looked, marching along with all the others in the afternoon heat. About to dismiss her as one more example of grim capitulation, he suddenly realised who she was.

Marni.

He said her name under his breath, overwhelmed by the feelings it brought up. How different she looked, having lost the independent air she once had, the sense of privilege that comes from money. Her father had lost everything after the coup, including his right to sit on the Sector Trading Committee because of certain views he'd expressed against the new government. But what was she doing here, caught up with the masses?

She stopped on the corner, as the faceless mob trudged past; she appeared to hesitate, detached from the mass of humanity that only moments ago she'd been a part of. Head erect, mouth set in a determined pout, she stood as a symbol of defiance, resolution.

Even under torture she'd revealed nothing. Harris himself had come to a grudging admiration for the courage she'd shown after days of interrogation. Seeing her now he felt a tinge of regret. Perhaps the biggest mistake he'd made was to sign her release papers.

As if sensing his scrutiny, she looked up, her gaze fixed in Harris' direction. His first instinct was to pull back to avoid being seen. Instead, gripped by a profound curiosity, he stared back. Was this a deliberate attempt by her to establish contact, to intimidate him in some way? And if so, how had she discovered his hideaway?

Then she was gone, re-joining the still moving throng. Harris remained at the window, overcome with an awful presentiment. The only person who knew of his whereabouts was Sorensen, and he was out of the country. They'd always been cautious, communicating only when necessary, using dead drops, and the occasional coded telephone call. Seeing Marni had been a coincidence. His mind playing tricks.

The exercise hour finished, and the street returned to its former condition, sullen and brooding. Even the crow had gone, flying off to some other sector. Out of all the inhabitants of the city, only the birds were truly free, looking down on their human counterparts with bemused indifference.

He took to his bed again – one more habit he found hard to break. The view of the ceiling allowed him to think and reflect, to plan his next move. All the subjects under the sun, collected there alongside the cracks in the plaster and strips of peeling paint: the mystery of life and death, and the irreversible nature of time; the nagging ache for a woman that never really went away. Countless hours and minutes spent alone in this one room, with its sparse furnishings and stale air, an endless desert from which there was no escape.

The image of Marni disturbed him. Her lone figure on the street corner. The pale spectre of her face, and the inescapable impression that she was trying to communicate something to him. The past, unfolding before him like one of the government processions that passed along the main square.

The painting on the wall caught his eye: a cheap print depicting a family sitting at a rustic wooden table. The man and wife looked on as their two children dipped bread into bowls of broth, while chickens foraged for scraps in the courtyard. The picture had an odd appeal, harking back to some idealised vision of a world that might once have existed. Harris' own family on their hundred-acre estate with stables and a lake. His Russian born wife, elegant and aloof, whose impeccable breeding and political connections were thrown in as part of the deal when they were married.

How quickly his star had risen, with all the various elements in place; his defection and integration into the system; the promise of a new life in exchange for classified information. How soon it had all come tumbling in on him. His wife. The estate. All gone in a matter of months. He learned what it was like to be without friends. To find his luck had finally run out, in this the deadliest of games.

I could kill myself, he thought. All I have to do is open the window and leap out. Self-preservation and cowardice prevented such a move, but the thought persisted. Despair set in instead, the kind prisoners feel when hope is abandoned and the reality of the situation becomes apparent.

The low murmur of a vehicle disturbed his reverie.

Lying there, listening out, a wave of fear engulfed him. The only vehicles permitted in the area were those of the regular patrols that cruised the streets looking for criminals, or those who defied the curfew. They must be coming for him, tipped-off by one of the residents in the block, who'd discovered his true identity.

A door slammed shut, then another. Footsteps echoed on the street below. Then voices, indistinct, but charged with excitement, anticipation.

He hurried to the window and looked out. Sure enough, there in the street below was the ominous grey façade of a patrol vehicle, its side panel flecked with dust. The driver idled behind the wheel, the engine ticking over. Two government agents in plain clothes strode purposefully towards the entrance to the adjacent apartment block. They wore the standard poor quality suits, and hats angled on their heads in a mock stylish manner. Their combined menace had a kind of blandness to it, like an unpolished veneer.

One of them pressed a buzzer on the intercom system, and they waited, scanning the empty street for any signs of movement. They shuffled their feet and remained vigilant, eager to carry out their sinister task.

The door to the building opened, and they slipped inside, leaving the driver in the vehicle with the engine running.

Harris stepped back from the window to avoid being seen; curiosity could get you killed, or earn you ten-years in a labour camp just for being in the wrong place. But this was a piece of theatre, an unexpected late-afternoon performance that broke up the serial monotony and added an element of uncertainty to the proceedings. They were all players in a drama that had no beginning and no end. The government agents and the poor unfortunates they persecuted, soon to be taken from their place of safety to an interrogation room deep in the bowels of the city – and from there to God only knew where. Many simply disappeared and were never seen again.

Like a virus, the fear intensified, leading his thoughts to areas too bleak to contemplate. And yet, mixed with this, a kind of excitement also. Senses, dulled by the routine of daily life, came alive as if awakened from a long sleep. Sounds were amplified, thrown up from the street below through the open window. Snapshots of his previous incarnation, in a role not unlike theirs, stalking his quarry sometimes for weeks at a time. The details he was given were often scant – perhaps a photograph or an address, a single clue which could be built upon gradually. Then the final act, the denouement, the part he enjoyed most of all: using his wits and expertise against those of his adversary.

The two government agents came out of the building with a man wearing factory worker's garb – loose-fitting blue overalls and an off-white undershirt buttoned at the neck. The man appeared to be calm, not under any physical constraint, and walked the short distance to the waiting vehicle without hesitation. The look was familiar, seen on the faces of prisoners who'd accepted their predicament and had prepared themselves stoically for what might come next.

Then they were gone. The last rumble of the vehicle's engine died away and the street was quiet again. Harris stayed at the window, gazing down at the street. Nothing else stirred; the oppressive heat had sucked all the oxygen from the air and left a vacuum. The proles hid in their apartments, afraid to come out. And yet he couldn't blame them, for they too were victims of a conjuring trick, the propaganda machine that'd duped the whole country.

Still no word from Sorensen. Their weekly phone calls had ceased abruptly; an automated message informing Harris that the number he'd dialled was unrecognised. No guarantee Sorensen was still alive, such was the level of disruption and chaos brought about by the coup. But Sorensen was his only hope of getting across the border, and escaping the wolf pack committed to hunting him down.

Trapped here he was as good as dead, his life measured out in torturously slow seconds. Better to leave now and take his chances in the backstreets where the militia were less likely to go. And yet, to abandon this one room and venture outside meant even greater risk. To stay meant stagnation and uncertainty, but also a strange kind of solace. The room had been his sanctuary *and* his prison, ever since his face had appeared on one of the nightly news bulletins that went out across the city. The only jailors here were the doubts and fears conjured up by his own mind, but like the agents who hid in the shadows, these too were relentless.

Movement outside: the giveaway creak of floorboards in the hallway.

Creeping over to the door, he listened. Unable to discern any movement, he opened it and peered through the crack.

Standing there, with a look of solemn innocence, was the little girl who lived with her mother in a room along the hall. Hanging limply in her arms was an oversized cat, which she talked to soothingly like an adult to a child.

The little girl looked up at him through the gap in the doorway.

'He keeps running away from me,' she said.

He opened the door a little wider; no sounds came from the hallway, or the floors below.

'Where's your mother?'

'Working.'

She kissed the cat's head, observing Harris evenly.

'A lady asked me about you.'

'What lady?'

The little girl shrugged; the cat's hind legs kicked in a futile bid to escape.

'What did she look like?' he said. 'It's important you remember.'

'She was tall, with dark hair and dark eyes.'

Harris froze, the vague description confirming his fears.

'What did she ask you?'

'She showed me a photograph of a man who looked like you, and asked me if you lived here.'

'And what did you tell her?'

'I said I'd never seen anyone who looked like that before.'

He turned to go, alert now to a myriad possibilities.

'I need some money to buy food for the cat. Could you help me, please?'

He reached into his pocket for some change. The girl weighed it in the palm of her hand, unimpressed. He both admired and feared her at the same time. A child, trained to observe the smallest of details, and to pass them on to someone in a position of authority.

Closing the door, he took a deep breath. The girl had no idea who he was, or what he was hiding from. Her mother worked long hours at the glass factory and was rarely seen; they'd hardly spoken, except to exchange the odd pleasantry. But the message was clear. His hiding place had been compromised. To make good his escape, he had to act now. Leave this prison cell with its view of the drab apartment blocks across the street, and head for the border.

Packing a small bag, he took only a few essentials: a change of clothes, the gold ingots he could use to barter with, and the small seven-shot revolver Sorensen had given him before they'd parted the last time. The butt felt comfortable in his palm, instilling a sense of power and confidence.

Slipping out quietly, he vacated his room for the last time. Down the stairs to the rear exit, where he was less likely to be seen. Then out into the street, where the open space overwhelmed him.

The first time he'd been out for days, and the feeling of danger grew even stronger.

He longed for the safety of his room, and the protection of four walls. Conflicting thoughts assailed him. Maybe the little girl along the hall was a spy for the government. She would report back everything she saw to her mother, who would pass the details on in return for subsistence payments and transport tokens. Everything a threat in one form or another, even the deserted streets that promised the escape he craved.

A car pulled alongside; it had the official chequered emblem of the municipal taxi rank – the only company licensed to operate in the city. He recognised the driver, a man who lived in the next block, and was known to have partisan sympathies.

Leaning over, the driver addressed Harris through the open window.

'You want a lift?'

A glance at his watch confirmed the time – just after seven. With luck he could make the outskirts of the city before the eight o'clock curfew.

'I don't have much money.'

'That's OK, jump in.'

Life seemed to hinge on simple decisions that could have grave consequences if an error of judgement was made. Reading the driver's expression he saw nothing suspicious, more an unspoken urgency that he ought to comply. The taxi offered anonymity and relative safety. But to where? Other questions arose. What were the driver's motives, and why the sudden act of charity? Had he seen Harris' face on one of the news bulletins and was aware of his background?

On a whim, he climbed in the passenger side, and shut the door; a heady mix of worn leather and body odour assailed him immediately. But more than this, the sensation of being trapped within the confines of the car, at the mercy of elements beyond his control.

'Where are you heading?' the driver said.

'To the outskirts.'

'Sector 9?'

The reference alarmed him, such a prohibited place mentioned so carelessly, as if it were an ordinary street in the city. By admitting that this was his intended destination he was putting himself at even more risk, but there seemed no other way.

'Can you take me there?' Harris said.

'Sure. No problem.'

Sector 9 had an almost mythical status among the recidivists, those who lived on the margins of society and wished to remain hidden. How he would be received there was another matter, but he had to see it through.

They drove the two miles or so to the outskirts, past the oil refinery and the steelyard that had shut down months ago. The taxi driver drove smoothly, within the speed limit, the radio playing popular music in the background. He talked about his family, and how his brother had been sentenced to ten years hard labour for distributing anti-government literature. It was worse now, he said. The government had a stranglehold on the city. The people were like sheep herded into pens, afraid to speak out and unable to think for themselves.

Something about the driver's manner didn't seem right. He was too open, too willing to disclose potentially dangerous information about himself and his family. Experience told Harris to be cautious, not to say anything that might implicate him if they were stopped.

'You must know Koppel?' Harris said, making conversation. 'He's pretty big in the underground movement now, so I hear.'

The driver nodded emphatically, pleased to have found a common ground.

'Koppel. Yes, I know him. I saw him only last week at the Exchange.'

A sign gave the distance as a mile remaining to the city limits. Harris felt a surge of hope. All he had to do was find the right people in Sector 9, and use the gold ingots to obtain false papers.

From there he could get across the border and build a new identity.

'What's that?' he said, startled.

Up ahead, the familiar outline of a barrier blocking the road. Two stationary vehicles were parked at the roadside. Standing beside them, two armed militia, distinctive in their long coats and peaked caps.

'A roadblock?' Harris said. 'Out here?'

'Just routine. You have papers?'

A sense of unease stirred. The driver's reaction seemed a little too blasé, his tone conversational, unperturbed.

Harris made a decision.

'Pull over.'

The driver looked surprised, as if this wasn't part of the plan.

'Are you sure?'

'Just do it.'

The driver pulled over on the side of the road. Chain-link fencing divided the highway from a wide open tract of land. Rusted oil drums and old machinery parts lay scattered around like carcasses. Beyond this, the white lights that ringed the industrial sector, giving the buildings inside an unnatural glow.

'What will you do now?' the driver said. 'There's nowhere to go.'

Harris reached into the bag, his fingers closing around the butt of the revolver. He pictured the entry wound in the driver's forehead, the look of shock on his face.

Engines coughed into life somewhere behind him. Headlight beams lit up the road. Two vehicles accelerated out from a gap in the chain-link fencing, and raced towards him.

Unable to respond quickly enough, Harris was caught, halfway out of the passenger side. The two vehicles converged on the taxi, screeching to a stop. Men in plain clothes leapt out, aiming revolvers at him. From the exultant looks on their faces he knew they weren't militia.

They grabbed him, and marched him to the side of the road. He made no attempt to escape, or to offer resistance. The whole thing had been carried out smoothly and effectively, an operation he might even have ordered himself in his previous role.

Passing one of the vehicles, he noted a shadowy figure on the back seat. Peering closer, he saw the man's face, pale and gaunt, eyes bloodshot but dulled from exhaustion.

One more element revealed. Sorensen had obviously been arrested and had given him up. And yet something else bothered him.

'Have you managed to work it out?'

Startled, he turned to see Marni standing by one of the stationary vehicles. She had a look of victory.

'You almost made it,' she said. 'You must be so disappointed.'

He saw it clearly. The little girl cradling the cat in the hallway. The language of betrayal affecting everyone.

'Can we negotiate?' he said. 'I must be worth more to you alive than dead, surely?'

She shook her head, the faintest hint of amusement.

'You have nothing left to negotiate with. Too many good people died because of you.'

She gave a nod to the armed men, who forced Harris to his knees. An acute awareness kicked-in. His peripheral vision expanded. The bogus militiamen removed the barrier from the road, a stage prop no longer needed.

Looking up, he beheld the night sky, a thing of beauty, majesty. The white lights along the industrial section seemed unusually bright. He felt calm, as if all his earthly problems had ceased to be. Now he could finally stop running.

Somewhere In Nebraska

'All men are destined to die, but some die barely having lived at all.' He couldn't remember where the saying came from, but it seemed appropriate for this particular moment. June 6, 1944 – a brief flicker in history that would be analysed and commented on for decades to come. The casualties so far were too depressing to think about, many of them not even making it out of the landing craft and on to the appointed beachhead. Young men, many of them still in their teens, cut down by the German machineguns strung out along the cliffs. The rest scattered across the sand, exposed, desperate for protection from the relentless fire.

Reports from the other landing zones were more optimistic. The heavy concentration of troops, combined with the speed and accuracy of the attack, had made it hard for the Germans to counter. Hitler had been caught sleeping, literally, his generals fooled into thinking the spearhead would come further north. An impressive coup for British Intelligence, which'd certainly done its research. Eighteen months of planning since Eisenhower's initial forays along the French coast, then the big push. Normandy, and the five crucial beachheads which could make or break the entire operation: Juno, Sword, Gold, Utah and Omaha, the last of which would be forever associated with mayhem and disaster.

A student of Clausewitz might've remarked on the cost in terms of lives lost and ground gained. Had the sole objective been to liberate Paris, and secure the relevant bridges across the sector, then a percentage of losses would've been deemed acceptable, an unavoidable consequence of war. But the sheer scale of the operation made the outcome impossible to predict. The British did things in their own way, always pragmatic and outwardly unemotional – perhaps a little too cautious at times. This, however, was beyond anyone's comprehension. If the heavy casualties from the combined Allied assault meant anything at all, the officers and the chiefs of staff would never show it. Nothing could interfere with the overall plan – to liberate Europe and defeat the Germans.

The letter from home added to the general confusion. Reading it again in the poor light from a kerosene lamp brought back the same feelings. The tests from the hospital had come back negative, Marta said, but the doctor had suggested a further investigation to see if they could find out more. Her symptoms were perplexing – the fatigue and the aching joints, the sickness that confined her to bed for days on end. Of course, all this should've been secondary to his own predicament right now, but it was hard to make the distinction. And Marta's attempts to downplay the seriousness only made it worse. What could he do to help her, stuck out here with a drama all of his own?

He folded the letter, and slipped it back in the envelope. Home was a dream, a collection of images he rarely allowed himself to dwell upon. Death and suffering had come to so many under his command that he'd foregone the right to reminisce. Responsibility came at a huge price. No matter how you reasoned with yourself, you couldn't quite get over the guilt attached, the persistent feeling that you should've been taken too, and your personal effects shipped back home.

Lieutenant Deever poked his head through the tent flaps, like a character in one of the camp shows that entertained the men.

With his horn-rimmed glasses and bookish air, he had the look of a cleric. The army didn't suit his disposition, but like all natural survivors, he'd found an area he could excel at – in this instance, the collecting and disseminating of vital pieces of information, unearthed from one obscure source or another. Even the ever-growing numbers of the dead had some profound statistical relevance for him, as he attempted to discharge his obligations whenever and wherever he could.

Deever stepped inside, and saluted stiffly. Their close proximity over the preceding months had led to an uneasy familiarity between them, a blurring of professional lines that might in other circumstances have loosely been called a 'friendship.' But lately, Deever's presence inspired an irritation, as if he'd adapted his role purely for this purpose.

'Sir, I've just received information that the village has been taken, and the draw is now open. Engineers have blown the walls, and the road is clear of debris.'

'Are all the beaches clear now?'

'We're getting conflicting reports, but it looks like Gold and Juno are clear. I'm currently waiting on updates from the 29th and 1st Infantry, which I will duly pass on.'

Deever was a pedant. You could hear it in his voice, his choice of certain words, which he rolled off his tongue with a perverse pleasure. These small, otherwise inconsequential habits of his had taken on a major significance as the campaign dragged on; the way he slurped his coffee from the standard army-issue tin mug, his thin lips poised above the rim; the insane humming he did occasionally to some obscure tune, like a fly trapped in an airless room.

'Do you need me for anything else, sir?'

'Let me know when they've cleared the beaches.'

Deever looked disappointed, hoping for something else to do. Then, with a sharp salute, he exited through the tent flaps and was gone.

The news was encouraging, especially the capture of Vierville-sur-Mer, and the crucial draw leading up from the beach. The

Germans had commanded the high ground, able to rake the shoreline with their lethal MG 42s, pounding the Allied positions with howitzers and rockets. No one had expected it to be an easy campaign, but the troops packed into the Higgins boats never had a chance. The taking of Vierville was a start, the beginning of an offensive that would swing the balance of the war.

Secrecy, the key word. Months of planning that resulted in co-ordinated landings along the French coast. Nothing like it in military history to compare. And yet, out of all that, human error on a major scale which had dire consequences. Initial bombing runs that missed the target, dropping their loads onto fields and woodland, leaving the German guns free to do their damage. The terrible cost that followed – especially in the companies unlucky enough to have landed on Omaha that morning. Young boys of the 1st and 29th, many of them barely out of high school, whose first taste of combat would also be their last. Perhaps the nearest equivalent had been the mad scramble over the trenches at the Somme and Passchendaele, right into swathes of enemy fire. Thousands of men sacrificed for a few feet of ground. Now US Military had its own makeshift graveyard to rank alongside the great slaughterhouses of the past. 'Easy Red' and 'Fox Green', two sectors along a 5-mile stretch of coastline, awash with the blood of the dead.

Distant gunfire carried over on the coastal breeze, reminding him he was still in a war zone. Mistakes were made, even by the best of men, who prided themselves on their superior tactics. The Romans at Cannae, lured into a trap by Hannibal's forces: lacking real leadership at the front, the legions had marched into what should've been an easily detectable feint, only to be surrounded by flanking cavalry, cut-off from any possible retreat. Caesar would never have permitted such a fatal mistake, even with his own tendency to recklessness now and then.

Any study of history revealed the flaws in man's thinking, his rapaciousness and greed. And yet, out of all of this came tremendous examples of courage and sacrifice.

Now Henderson.

The obligation filled him with dread. As commanding officer, he couldn't evade the task – a few kind words of sympathy for the loss of someone he'd met only briefly and didn't particularly like that much. Henderson was an enigma, opinionated and loud-mouthed, always stirring up some form of trouble, and yet he'd always been popular with the men of the 16th.

Now, with his bloated corpse washed-up on Omaha Beach, there could only be a token reflection and a feeling of regret. One of the thousands fated never to make it ashore, Henderson's contribution to the assault would be a case of misfortune rather than personal valour. But he too would be remembered and honoured among the dead.

The first words were the hardest. After that, it became easier, just a matter of following the dictates of protocol.

'Dear Mrs Henderson, it is with regret that I have to inform you ...'

The two kids he'd left behind would grow up thinking their father had been a war hero, one of so many who'd given their lives for the common good. He pictured Mrs Henderson as a harassed housewife, yelling at her kids from her hand painted stoop, somewhere in Nebraska. In this idealised and All-American version, she wore a summer dress and had her hair up in a bun. An attractive woman, she'd probably been a source of pride to her husband, as they jived on the local dance floor before he got shipped out. Now she was a widow, a victim of the army's ineptitude, joining thousands just like her all across the country.

War relegated all things secondary to its single mercenary end. And yet he could've educated Mrs Henderson as to its essential nature, and given her examples as to its necessity for the survival and ongoing prosperity of man. Whenever a period of peace lasted too long the struggle for dominance reasserted itself. Then, like the changing of seasons, war came along to break up the status quo and force change. But you couldn't tell that to the wives and mothers who'd lost the ones they loved, whose only essence remained in memories and photographs.

The letter took longer than he thought. Fatigue crept over him, the result of lack of sleep – the regular bombardment of the senses, both literally and figuratively. Henderson's worries were over, his brief tenure here on earth given up. How absurd it seemed, that someone so vocal in life, and so committed to his own viewpoint, had been silenced forever by an unseen enemy. The German machine-gunners dug into the clifftop knew nothing of Henderson or his objectionable personality. Death was neutral, arbitrary, seeking no one in particular as its victim, but always closed to any negotiation in that respect. The corpses floating in the shallow water were faceless, lacking the discernible features that distinguished them when they were alive. Death rendered them all equal, the privates and the officers alike. And yet, the thought of Henderson's animated features, all lit-up at some perceived slight, prompted an unexpected wave of compassion. Too late to go back and change anything. The letter was the least he could do.

Deever poked his head through the flaps, and saluted stiffly. Deever the academic, his pale, bespectacled form unsuited to the rigours of battle.

'Sir, intelligence reports say the beachhead is now secured. But we're still taking prisoners, some Polish and Russian, from what we can make out. What should we do with them all?'

'Hand them over to the military police. That's their job, let them deal with it.'

The news failed to elicit the response Deever was looking for. He stood inside the tent, waiting for further instructions, eye wide, as if perpetually adjusting to the light.

'Do you have family at home, Deever?' A question he'd never asked before, that seemed to take on a new significance.

'I do, yes, sir.' Deever blinked rapidly, a flicker of unease he tried to hide.

'You have a wife – children?'

'No, sir. I live with my mother on Long Island.'

Reference to the homeland, to another time and place. A visit to New York and Connecticut with Marta in the Fall one year, an occasion that now seemed unbearable to even think about.

'Shall I notify the rest of the company, sir?'

'Tell them to strike camp and join the other units out on the main road. We'll head inland and link up with the 101st.'

'Is there anything else, sir?'

'That'll be all.'

With a sharp, almost comical salute, Deever exited, keen to carry out his latest assignment. Soon the military machine would be on the move, like a great beast awakening from its temporary sojourn to join the Allied forces further on up the road. A sense of inevitability had seized upon them collectively, an urgent whisper in the ear of every soldier in every platoon. Soon, Paris would be liberated. From there, anything was possible.

He went over the letter once more, looking for any mistakes and inconsistencies, unintended slights. Always an element of hypocrisy in every line – the blandness of officialdom, attempting words of condolence on official government notepaper. Wives and mothers, informed of their sons' noble sacrifice, a task the military hierarchy just wasn't qualified for. The letter would arrive by post, belatedly, received by Mrs Henderson on that same hand painted stoop, somewhere in Nebraska, its contents unable to anticipate the enormity of her loss, or offer any real comfort at all. And to the author of these futile missives, there could be no sense of closure, only a partial relief that the job was finally over. One more body bag on its way home.

Putting the letter aside, he turned to a fresh page, this time on his own personal notepaper. Kneading his brow, he closed his eyes and allowed his mind to wander. Home seemed an impossibly long distance away, a conundrum of time and space. Sometimes he had to look at a photograph to remind him what Marta looked like, to reassure himself of the connection they still had. Questions naturally arose. Did she miss him as much as he missed her? Did she count down the days and weeks and months until he'd be home again, and they could resume the life they'd lived before he went away? It didn't pay to get too sentimental, to allow yourself the luxury of reflection when there was still so much to do. War required a different perspective, a deliberate blunting of the usual range of emotions in order to meet the many challenges you had to face. And yet, buried deep within him was that yearning for closeness and intimacy, the special bond that had developed between them over the years and grown stronger over time.

A distant burst of artillery fire brought him back to the present moment, a reminder that the invasion was far from over. Hard to find the words to say how he felt. The enormity of the losses on the beach. So many healthy young men, the hopes and expectations of a long life before them. Marta wouldn't understand. Civilians never did. War changed you in ways you couldn't explain. You saw things you couldn't talk about to anyone else – including those you drank with and ate with, sharing the pressures of leadership that came with its own anxieties. And yet the real enemy was always yourself, some aspect of your character that wasn't up to the job and would always catch you out.

Later, he took a stroll down onto the beach with Deever, to assess the carnage. The man-made sea walls and defensive positions were still in place, but the bodies were gone, removed by the clean-up operation that followed. Everywhere, evidence of what looked like a mass exodus: discarded pieces of equipment strewn across the sand; radios and shell casings, the burnt-out hulks of amphibious tanks, most of which hadn't made it out of the water.

Looking up at the cliffs, he could see the bunker positions that'd housed the German machineguns, giving them lethal coverage of the troops in the landing crafts. Many soldiers had drowned, unable to extricate themselves from their heavy backpacks, as they floundered in the water. Those that did manage to stagger ashore had found precious little shelter from the crossfire. No foxholes to take shelter in, and no aerial bombardment to take out the guns.

He found a set of dog-tags lying in the sand, the links broken, as if torn from the wearer's neck in a moment's trauma. Etched into the tin plate, clearly visible, was the name, *Private Estevez, Ramon*, followed by the service number, blood type and religion. The find unsettled him, as if he was meant to stumble across this *momento mori* on such a desolate stretch.

Deever joined him, peering over at the dog tags in his hand.

'I don't think there's much else we can do here, sir. Should we head back?'

Perhaps they shared the guilt of those who'd come through unscathed, having been spared the fate of the men on the beach. The dog tags were a grim reminder.

He handed them to Deever, who stared at them, bemused.

'See that these are shipped back to private Estevez's family.'

'Yes, sir.'

Beyond the beach lay the sea, the casual wash of the surf along the shore almost peaceful now. Nature, indifferent to the slaughter that had taken place only hours before. The blood of so many, offered up as a sacrifice to a just cause, now dissolved in the ocean.

Aware of Deever beside him, he straightened up and assumed his former bearing. Not good to show weakness of any kind to a subordinate, especially one with Deever's analytical mind. And yet the moment called for some form of acknowledgement, a kind of requiem, even if it had to remain unspoken.

Together they strolled back through the sand, the tall cliffs to their right, now just another part of the scenery. Hard to believe that this isolated stretch of beach had formed the basis for the entire operation. A 60-mile landing zone from Caen to the eastern side of Cherbourg, the men of the US 1st Infantry Division leading the way.

Like Henderson, private Estevez would also have a family. The dog tags were all that was left of him, a treasured possession for a wife or mother. But to the military department, he would always be a statistic, a number. Private Estevez, R. Born to die on Omaha Beach.

The worst was over – at least for now. All that was left was hope, a dim flicker on the far horizon.

Animation

The steel shutter closed just as the lights went out across the world. The lock snapped back into place, the impact echoing out along the mezzanine.

Silence.

The walkway came out of the gloom, caught in the thin white beam of the headset: glass-fronted stores with archaic names like 'Empire Travel' and 'Phone Warehouse.' An underground tomb filled with relics from the past, all preserved as they had been before the big closure.

Strange visuals up ahead. A poster in a window – a laughing couple and small child in a sun-drenched meadow. The man had blonde hair and a natural smile. The woman had long platinum hair infused with sunlight, and soft red lips curled over perfect white teeth. The child gazed up at them in awe. Their innocence projected a certain image, a way of life no longer valid under the new regime.

The picture stirred a memory deep inside. She had no idea who the couple and child were, only that they were all that was left of the old way. A poster in an underground city behind steel shutters, off-limits to anyone without a pass. And yet they represented something alluring and forbidden, a world of colour and light, of endless choice.

She made contact with the control centre, and gave her location. The response came back automatically. *Proceed and identify target.*

Heading along the 'tunnel', a cold, forbidding place full of shadows and reflections, she ran the coordinates through the computer. Vague images stared back from darkened shop windows, the probing beam from her headset lighting up the interiors. She caught her own reflection in the plate glass. The remodelled contours of her face, that'd replaced the less expressive features of the old version. This was her new look, her new function. Female android G-17. Programmed to lure and seek out fugitives in order for them to be destroyed.

More anomalies further along. Behind the window of one emporium, strange life-size figures dressed in outdated clothing. They stared out, bald-headed and sightless, without any distinguishing features. Like the couple and the child in the poster they too were trapped here in this mausoleum, unseeing and forgotten, illuminated briefly in her headset beam. In some ways they resembled the first prototypes built by the scientists at N-Corp. But these were different; they had no neural circuitry, no language and problem-solving ability. All they did was replicate humans in appearance only.

At the end of the tunnel was a double door marked 'No Admittance.' She pushed against the bar, and the doors crashed open. Beyond, lay another corridor. A wall light flickered, partially lighting the way ahead. Water dripped from the abutment, staining the surface of the wall a slimy black. She stopped to check the screen, making sure she was heading in the right direction. According to her feed there should be a stairway up ahead, leading to an underground car park. Beyond that, a stadium which had once been used for entertainment.

The smooth mezzanine of the shopping mall gave way to rough concrete, uneven and gritty underfoot. The air was cooler here, as if stirred from some exterior source. Now and then she glanced behind her, aware that she was alone and vulnerable should anything happen. She could always call in the Sentinels, but it would take time for them to arrive, especially as they'd have to be dispatched by the control centre first. Closing down her communication system would leave the channels open for emergency calls only, but this would reduce the information coming in and leave her even more vulnerable. The entire area was prohibited to all but those who'd been authorised, left standing as a kind of museum piece, record of a time and place that was now obsolete. Her N-Corp pass wouldn't help her either. She'd simply be identified as an intruder and dealt with accordingly by those who'd taken refuge here.

A gloomy and dank stairwell led down to a small landing. So far, the directions she'd been given had been accurate, but an inner voice advised caution. Her footsteps were amplified in the small space, the sense of her own passage through the building heightened by the unearthly still that settled all around. And yet her sense of anticipation grew. To identify a target could mean promotion to another unit, and a possible transfer to the Free Zone where there were less restrictions. With 12 months to go until mandatory retirement, she had no other option, no safeguards in place. Current android models like hers could soon become obsolete themselves, superseded by new technology. But as a member of the elite Hunter Division she had prestige, the opportunity for advancement. In less than six months she'd become their most successful operative, having lured and identified more targets than any other model.

This one was different. He'd been given special status, a priority to all units in the field. All she had to do was find and identify him. The Sentinels would do the rest.

A doorway led to a spacious and gloomy labyrinth; concrete pillars set at intervals under a low ceiling. Dust particles caught in the beam of her headset light – inert and lifeless in the haze. Everything abandoned and without purpose. A series of bays were marked out, the spaces divided by white lines. Most of the bays were empty, but in some were ancient vehicles, their windows blacked-out. They gave the place an odd feeling of habitation, that once there might have been life and movement here, the transit of vast numbers of people, who once relied on these strange lumps of metal to transport them across the city.

Peering through the window of one, she could just make out the interior: cracked and worn leather seats, an over-large steering wheel with a leopard print cover. Hanging from the rear-view mirror was a talisman of some kind: a round yellow face, with two dots for eyes and a smiling mouth. Her archive feed gave the year of the model and the history. *Citroen C3 Hatchback, 2010.* She pictured the occupants, strapped in and moving through dense traffic on one of the city's vast highways. A family like the one in the poster, their journey punctuated with the sound of laughter and joy, frustration and sorrow. Emotional responses no longer valid under the new regime.

Two options flashed up on her screen: *Save*, or *Delete*. For some obscure reason she chose Save, and stored the document in a folder with all the others. The rules forbade the storage of unapproved material, but in this case she could claim it was attached to the search for the target, making it a legitimate source.

A noise from the shadows.

The steady drip of water into a nearby pool.

She trained the headset beam into the dark corners, to flush out any potential assailant. Nothing registered on the screen, other than the dust particles and concrete pillars, the inert vehicles in the bays. But something else was out there. She knew this instinctively.

The headset beam probed the shadows, lighting up the parapet on the other side. Something moved, indistinct, hidden by the concrete pillars.

Then it registered on her screen, a faint silhouette, matching her stride for stride. She recognised the pattern, the soft, blue light at the extremities that gave the impression of a moving force field; any facial features were obscured by the poor light.

The figure's movement over the concrete made no sound at all. But her thermal imaging picked up the body heat, definitive proof that the image was human, marked for elimination. Here also were clear markers of the subject's pathology: a history of tooth decay in childhood; inflammation around a broken femur which had never fully healed. Age estimated at around thirty.

Alarmed, she stayed still, gauging the distance between them. None of this was in the original plan – one swift reconnoitre of the forbidden place, then report back to the control centre, where she could hand over the assignment and sign out. This was unexpected, beyond the limits of her programming. There weren't supposed to be any survivors left at all; they were supposed to have been eliminated during the last purge. But she'd fed all the details into the computer and it had come up with the location. Could it be that by hiding down here in the Prohibited Zone they'd found a way to survive without detection?

Readjusting her headset beam, she made out his face – or at least an essence of it. Automatic Face Recognition scanned thousands of likenesses, but no match was found. Something else came up instead. His power source was down, evident in the weakness of the signal transmitted; the reason she might not have picked it up originally. His features were also unclear; the eyes dimmed and set back, the mouth partly open, signifying pain or distress of some kind.

Forced to make a decision, she opted to leave him there. Pushing open the door marked 'Exit', she entered the stairwell. The next logical move would be to call in her coordinates to the control centre, and let them dispatch the Sentinels. Instead, she kept going, compelled to see what might happen next.

The target followed.

She picked up her pace, along the passage that linked the mall to the concourse. Her archive feed flashed up more information. This was a place where humans had once congregated in large numbers. Unlike the shopping mall, this was an altogether different structure, a network of passages and arches that ran in an ellipses, with entrances set at intervals. The archive played a short clip on her screen. Thousands of spectators rose as one in a roar of excitement. They wore distinctive scarves and hats; banners and flags flew in a sea of colour. The programme was supposed to have erased all obsolete data from the system, and yet this had come up.

Then she realised why.

It wasn't the archive feed at all. The images were coming from somewhere else. From the target himself.

She headed for the stadium up ahead, confused, unsure which action to take. And there behind her, keeping his distance, was the target. His bluish aura lit up like neon in the gloom of the passageway. What if there were more like him? His lone presence was in fact a ruse to lure her deeper into the building?

Left with no alternative, she alerted the command centre.

Nothing came back.

She tried again. The connection failed a second time, leaving her alone and isolated. Now she was stuck with no back-up and no reception.

Still he followed, his shimmering aura giving him away. She sensed his weakness, that soon his energy levels would fade out altogether, forcing him to stop. But this one's ability to get away undetected aroused her curiosity. She wanted to know more about him. Where had he come from, and how had he managed to evade the Sentinels for so long? And why did he warrant such a special status?

Heading along the passage, she came to a set of turnstiles that would at one point have processed vast numbers of human beings. She'd read the histories and seen the files: homo sapiens – a species vulnerable to viruses and disease, motivated by destructive urges that constantly threatened their survival. The Centre for Evolutionary Studies called this trait a 'regrettable flaw that could not be allowed to persist.' The new way held the old accountable. All inferior life forms were to be phased out over a specific time period. Under the new edicts, child-birth and old age would no longer exist, eradicating age-old problems of hunger, disease and global conflict. Artificial Intelligence had eliminated the potential for human error and made existence more predictable.

A barred door opened onto a vast arena, its banked sides containing rows of vacant bright red bucket seats. In the centre was a long rectangle of grass, overgrown with weeds. Her readout said that this was once a place where people assembled to watch licensed spectacles. Vast crowds cheering events that must've taken place right where she was standing.

Movement on the far side.

The target appeared at a tunnel-like entrance beneath the banks of seating. He observed her casually, under no constraint. She tried to access her security system, but again it failed to respond.

He started walking towards her across the grass. Closer now, she could see him clearly, and marvelled at the intricacies of his design. His face resembled that of the earlier species, before the introduction of the synthetic system. In spite of his weakened pulse, his eyes were clear and focussed. No outward signs of fear or alarm.

More details flashed up on her screen. This particular model had been phased out when the new series had become available. The old flesh and blood systems, which had been in existence for thousands of years, were outlawed and given obsolete status. The new synthetic systems weren't as prone to breaking down, and could be controlled from a central location. And yet here it was now, registering on her screen. The unmistakable signs of human life.

Abandoning his previous caution, he stepped towards her, and put up his hand – palm facing her. Guided by a force she didn't recognise, she raised her own hand and held it there, inches from his.

A prompt flashed up on her screen.

Connect?

Instinctively, she reached out and touched his palm; a ripple of electricity ran through her from head to toe as she accessed his power source. His eyes glowed a vibrant blue. For a second the outline of his face lit-up; his bone structure visible, like the pictures she'd seen in the history files and in the shopping mall. His facial features had a disconcerting autonomy, as if they moved with a life of their own independent of any programming.

Systems Connected!

His memory feed was now fully absorbed into hers, a shared

collection of thoughts and images. She saw him as he was before the model was phased out: a small child with parents, playing near the ocean, the surf washing his feet. Then later, playing with his friends in a park. Each new image stirred something inside her, the sense of a past she'd never experienced that somehow held some deeper significance. This stadium they were in was a place he used to go, before the first purge; she saw him as a child, seated in the crowd alongside his father. His memory feed showed his parents, a couple like the ones in the mall. They stood over him, smiling, as he played at their feet. Before the end of birth and death, the phasing out of procreation.

He took her hand, and guided her further into the arena. The roar of the crowd swelled around them, coming from some far-off place. This time the occasion was something different, played out on her screen in graphic detail. Thousands of humans filled the banked seats, and covered the rectangle of grass. A lone figure stood on a stage, holding a microphone. Tall and slender, with wavy blonde hair, she wore an electric blue dress that sparkled with sequins. Her presence seemed to stir the crowd to a collective ripple of appreciation, adoration even. The girl started to sing, a high plaintive note that soared aloft, lifting the entire stadium to its feet.

G-17 felt conflicted. Inside her, something she'd never experienced before. An awakening, a distant calling – the thing the teachers had warned against. The dangers of feeling and emotion that'd been phased out under the new regime. But she couldn't ignore her own reaction to the sensations the archive brought up. Absorbing the target's memory feed made it impossible, an experience she couldn't deny.

Onscreen, the singer performed for the crowd. An eerie semi-darkness had fallen over the auditorium. Thousands of tiny white lights shone from the vast audience like stars in the night sky. The singer implored them, arms outstretched, her voice rising higher. A solitary figure alone on the stage, she held her devotees transfixed through the sheer force of her personality.

The target's hand squeezed hers, a transferal of aural and

visual stimulation from one system to another. All the responses previously denied her under the new regime were now made available.

Desire

Excitement

Love

Questions arose naturally. Who was he, and how long had he been hiding? Were there others who had also escaped the deadline? But the answers no longer mattered, dissolved in a flood of warm feeling and wonder.

She understood why the survivors resisted the deadline, even at the risk of being hunted down. They were keeping alive an old, outdated system in order to preserve a prohibited way of life, one that contained limitless possibilities. She understood his desperation, knowing that his fate was somehow aligned with hers. The current technology would completely phase out the last remaining human characteristics in all species. The new synthetic models would make all the old, problematic behaviours redundant. Events like the concert she'd seen would no longer exist. Future generations would never experience the range of emotions available to the outdated human form. They would instead be digitised and pre-programmed, their reactions to life events controlled from a central source.

The singer's image flickered and faded on the screen. The target's signal grew weaker at the same time.

Blue to Green.

Still her hand in his, a simple reassurance.

A light going out.

His eyes sought hers in a silent plea. It was then that she realised who he was. The reason she'd been sent to lure him with her newly adopted female characteristics.

He was the leader. He'd escaped from one of the holding centres and gone underground, taking a small group with him. Over time their numbers had multiplied, defeating several government units sent against them. During this time he'd attained an almost mythical status, a symbol of hope to the ever diminishing bands of humans around the world.

Weakened by the sudden drain on her resources, her system struggled to cope. But her own wellbeing seemed less important. Now the target had given her something of infinite value. A dual heartbeat that could never be extinguished. A powerful spiritual component that could never be replicated by machines.

And yet, the old system had been outlawed for a reason. The human form in its natural state had proved to be too problematic, inciting wars and revolutions, and causing endless conflicts with its incessant demands. Leaders emerged, committed to their own selfish and often suicidal causes.

The question of her own future loomed. To stay here in this place with its connection to a past that no longer existed would be illogical. The target's weakened condition meant he was no real threat to her at all, in spite of his infamous reputation. Without her life force to sustain him he would simply wither and die.

But this would also be her fate. She too needed her system backed-up in order for her to remain alive.

Her feed flashed up a warning.

System compromised. Condition critical.

The target gazed into her eyes, a look of such intensity that it induced a response deep inside her. He squeezed her hand again, imparting a warm and sensual feeling. Now they were linked completely. They would go out together, like the lights strung across the auditorium. Each experiencing a range of prohibited emotions one last time.

A message came through from the control centre.

Communication re-established.

The control centre had picked up her alert, and were ready to deploy the Sentinels. All she had to do was give her coordinates.

Gazing up at the target beside her she made a decision. Releasing her hand from his, she stepped back. His face, once proud and noble, registered shock at first, then disappointment.

Relaying her coordinates to the control centre, she watched him slump further, visibly overcome.

Right away she felt better, stronger. Now that her system was no longer supporting his, her energy levels would soon be restored to their optimum level.

The Sentinels didn't take long.

A flash of polished body armour high above her. Familiar blacked-out visors that gave them away. They moved swiftly down the aisles between the empty bucket seats towards the arena.

The target remained motionless, refusing to respond. He stood erect, triumphant, energised by some unrecognisable source. His gaze met hers as if he'd known all along who she was. And she in turn felt something she'd never felt before. Sorrow. Grief. The part of her system that had merged briefly with his had left a lasting impression. She turned away, unable to look, as the Sentinels took him down.

Christ and the Devil

The Galilean went out into the desert. There in the wilderness, in the place called Jeshimon, where the dust lay baked upon the ground and the limestone formed jagged canyons all around, he prepared to meet his adversary. His feet ached from the length of the journey and the unyielding terrain, and all around him the wingtips of demons sent to deter him, emissaries of the dark forces that worked tirelessly for his destruction.

Weary and beleaguered on all sides, the Galilean chose a natural clearing to rest. Laying his worn sandals aside, he inspected his raw and blistered feet. This, then, was his fate, to share the burden of ordinary mortals – to suffer the indignity of physical pain and disillusion. The ancient prophets had foretold of the hardships he would face, and the temptations he would have to resist. These he faced with a deeply held conviction, an immovable sense of his own destiny. Here in the desert, with nothing but his scant clothing and great fortitude, he would continue to battle for the future of mankind.

For forty days and forty nights, the Galilean endured these

privations, consumed by hunger and discomfort, and the loneliness inspired by the desolate terrain. During this time, he called upon the Lord his God to sustain him and to give him the courage he needed. By day the heat scorched the earth. At night the cold settled in its place, the two extremes offering no relief. The demons circled, and such was their persistence that he could hear their laughter and feel their honey-sweet breath upon his cheek. Then, like the dust whipped up by the desert winds, they were gone, leaving him alone to ponder.

As the sun began its descent, a dust cloud appeared on the horizon, almost obscure to the naked eye. The Galilean looked closer. There it was, more distinct now, a swirling dance among the canyons, standing out from the dry carpet of earth studded with rocks and stone.

Then from the haze came a lone figure, striding purposefully in the Galilean's direction. A blood red cloak trailed behind him, visible against the scorched backdrop of the desert. Whatever guise this apparition came in, his real identity would soon be revealed, for he was known by several names in many languages. But to the Galilean he was Satan, the harbinger of destruction and enemy of truth.

Shielding his eyes from the sun, the Galilean beheld two winged cherubs, one either side of the approaching figure, their faces bathed in a rapture of delight. They babbled in tongues, as if to hasten the progress of their host, for they came from the same infernal place and could not contain their glee at this, the hour of reckoning.

Then Satan entered the place where the Galilean sat, and made a brief, preparatory circuit. Neither fatigued or disturbed by his long journey, he possessed instead an unnatural but palpable energy. At a signal, the cherubs took flight, carried off to await his instruction.

Now, alone within the circle marked loosely by stones, Satan cast his gaze down as if in deep reflection. When at last he spoke, his voice had all the coarseness and depth of the earth. But to temper this, he introduced a note of humour, a musical lilt most pleasing to the untrained ear.

'King of kings,' he said with a mocking bow. 'I hope you are sufficiently rested after your long journey?'

The Galilean thought before answering.

'I did not come here to rest or to seek comfort.'

'You came to the right place. Nothing grows here. All is dust and sand and heat.' Satan looked to the east, as if searching the horizon. His faint smile stayed fixed, in his eyes an essence of perverse pleasure.

The Galilean remained still, his composure untroubled. An aura of light surrounded him, animating his features, anointing his beard and long hair. A few spots of perspiration marked his brow, as the setting sun began its descent over the barren location. But his will had been weakened by his long fast, his ability to endure severely restricted.

Satan paced back and forth before him, like a Greek philosopher in the Forum at Rome; as if in contemplation of some perplexing dilemma. And yet, a sense of great anticipation seized him also, as if at the unfolding of a long-awaited story, a rich banquet he might lay at the feet of this, the King of kings.

Taking his leisurely stroll, red cloak trailing behind him, he glanced over at the seated Galilean, who remained subdued but dignified some feet away.

'It is said that you have miraculous powers,' Satan said. 'That you restore sight to the blind. How is it then, that one as eminent as you should have no servants? No slaves to wash the dust from your feet?'

'I have no need of such things, nor am I troubled by solitude.'

'How noble of you, to bear your trials alone.' Satan stopped pacing, and beheld the Galilean with interest. 'If you are who you say you are, why go hungry?' With a sweep of his hand, he gestured the cracked limestone that carpeted the earth. 'Turn these stones into bread.'

The Galilean stared into the periphery, where the evening shadows were starting to fall. From his long and solitary preparation, he had anticipated this moment, drawing from the well of strength provided for him by the Father. His lengthy desert vigil had brought about great visions, sunspots before his eyes, and the gnawing ache of hunger. The Lord his God had fortified him throughout this time, prepared him for this moment.

He answered Satan's challenge accordingly. 'It is written, Man shall not live by bread alone, but by every word that procedeth out of the mouth of God.'

At a signal from Satan, two slender young women stepped from the evening shadows like a mirage, each bearing a basket filled with succulent fruit and loaves of bread. They entered the enclosure, and put down their cargo before the Galilean, their gaze lowered in the manner of serving girls before a prince. But their outward bearing betrayed a certain mocking humour, for they too were fashioned from the same material as the winged cherubs, and came from the same dark place.

'There,' Satan said, with an expansive gesture. 'Let it not be said that I neglected my duties as host. Eat. Take your fill. End this pointless fast.'

The Galilean beheld the basket and its contents, and the women who stood back awaiting instructions. They raised their hooded eyes to gaze upon him with the same sly amusement as their host, the coils of copper bracelets at their wrists glinting in the fading light. And beholding the serpent among them, the Galilean declined.

Satan shook his head with apparent disappointment, and turning to the women, made a dismissive gesture. Without a word, they picked up the basket and headed back into the darkness from whence they came. Soon they were absorbed into the shadows, their slender outlines no longer discernible from the canyons of rock. For the darkness was now impenetrable, relieved only by the myriad stars in the night sky.

Alone with the Galilean once more, Satan once again took stock. Rather than be discouraged by the Galilean's obstinate stance, he seemed to take great pleasure from the outcome. His dominance was assured, a fact attested to by his confident demeanour, the enthusiasm he displayed in his role as master of ceremonies.

'I admire your resilience,' he said. 'To remain steadfast, even when the body is wracked with pain and hunger. This is worthy even of the Stoics.'

The Galilean said nothing, aware of his adversary some feet away – for each had maintained a respectful distance from the other. His adversary's voice had the same mocking charm, a lyrical quality that probed and teased, intending to draw him further into his web of lies.

Nightfall brought the cold, a bitter, freezing mantle that lay upon the desert. And yet the circle of rocks that contained them appeared illuminated, as if by torchlight. They remained as two players, cast upon this intimate space, one representing good, the other evil. All the pitfalls of humanity – the betrayals, the treachery, the lust and the greed were encapsulated and exalted in Satan's jubilant persona. For he had come from the dark place, heralded by trumpeters and charioteers, to begin the final battle for the souls of men.

'Come,' Satan said. 'I will show you all that awaits you. All the things that could be yours.'

With that the Galilean was swept up to a point upon which he could gaze down on the whole of Jerusalem. And here he beheld the Temple, from which all the laws were made, and all the edicts governing the tribes of the land.

Satan gestured with an outstretched hand, speaking in Hebrew, the Galilean's native tongue. 'If thou be the Son of God, cast thyself down: for it is written, He shall give his angels charge concerning thee: and in *their* hands they shall bear him up, lest at any time thou dash thy foot against a stone.'

The Galilean pondered his adversary's words, and replied thus:

'It is written again, thou shalt not tempt the Lord thy God.'

With that, Satan led the Galilean up to the highest point, where all the glittering palaces and temples were set out beneath them. Here were the cities of past, present and future, and all the inhabitants therein awaiting subjugation.

'Give your allegiance to me,' Satan said, 'and I will grant you the keys to all the cities in the world, and all the coffers of silver and gold.'

The Galilean gazed upon this sight with trepidation. The citadels sparkled like emeralds, conceived of and built by man. His defence lay in the scriptures, the words written long before by the holy men who foresaw his coming.

And yet, he balked. He saw an image of himself as a king seated on a throne, ruling over his subjects and granting favours like Caesar.

Gathering every ounce of resistance, he turned at once to his adversary.

'Away from me, Satan! For it is written. Thou shalt worship the Lord thy God, and him only shall thy serve.'

Once again, Satan's wishes were foiled. With a wave of his hand, the Temple heights and grand view of Jerusalem dissolved. The Galilean found himself back in the desert, to the circle of stones that formed the makeshift enclosure. And all he perceived there was all that had been before; and yet it appeared that the limestone and rock had taken on a different appearance, altered in both shape and form.

Satan paced back and forth before him, hands behind his back, taking slow, measured steps.

'It would appear that you have passed the tests set before you,' he said magnanimously. 'What will you do now?'

'Of myself I am nothing. The Father doeth all the work.'

'Such modesty from one whose claims are met with ridicule. Even now the Sanhedrin plot to rid themselves of you.'

'I fear not their accusations, or what they might do. I have been given strength for just such a purpose.'

'Strength alone will not save you. You will find nothing but pain and suffering at your appointed hour.'

'And when that hour comes I shall receive my Father's blessing, for this too is written.'

Satan laughed and shook his head. 'Your birth is cursed, like the fools you preach to. Even as we speak, the angels of darkness gather on the outskirts awaiting a sign from me. Then, and only then, will the scriptures be fulfilled, *as they were written.*'

Standing before the Galilean, Satan considered him carefully. A change came over him, subtle though it may have been. For one moment he seemed uncertain, almost overwhelmed by the taxing nature of his mission.

'Since we cannot agree upon a suitable resolution, I suggest a compromise,' he said. 'The lands to the east and west be divided equally between us. We in turn can govern as we see fit.'

The Galilean stood firm and unbending. 'There can be no such arrangement between us. You are the enemy of all that is good. I am the light to lead the way out of darkness.'

'But did not the armies of Saul defeat the Philistines, only to find their own lands divided? And did not Saul himself fall to the Amalekites, dying by his own hand in the midst of battle? What use is sovereignty when the king himself is dead?'

The Galilean pondered these words, knowing that they came with trickery and deceit.

'All men perish,' he said. 'Only those who come to the Father through me can know everlasting life.'

'But are we not two sides of the same coin?' Satan threw up his hands in the manner of a courtroom lawyer. 'You speak with authority, when in fact you have none. You are alone out here in this wilderness, without hope, and yet still you aspire to divine leadership.'

Satan took a step back, preparing his departure with a show of humility.

'Very well, you leave me little choice. I go now to prepare my forces. My generals and auxiliaries await me, for they are innumerable, and thirst for battle. But we shall meet again, in the hearts and minds of men and women – *as it is written.*

And so the two parted, Satan for his domain beyond the desert, the Galilean for his home in Judea. Between their two kingdoms ran a fast-flowing river that contained within it the essence of all life, where no thought or impulse could take root without being swept aside, and no illness or affliction could reside without being transformed into purest light. Into this river went the burdens of mankind and the divided nations of the earth, the profound essence of love and hate, the twin polarity of light and dark, and always the same relentless current flowing endlessly on for all time.

The Libertine

I have, of late, become aware of a strange regret stirring within me, and without much prompting on my part, it would seem. As I write these words, by the light of several candles and a meagre winter fire, the dogs are barking in the courtyard, perhaps at some petty disturbance among the kitchen staff; and the hall clock chimes melodically in a pleasant refrain. I sleep little these days, the early hours resembling a ghostly shroud under which I must lie, awaiting the first glimmer of dawn through the latticed window. Answering mail is perhaps the only discipline I have left – unless you count the daily excursions across the countryside on horseback accompanying the dogs, whose enthusiasm for the chase never wavers. This particular epistle arrived only yesterday, and required something of a cautious approach, bearing in mind the officious nature of its author. As I read on, I felt the stirrings of a strange premonition, that my somewhat turbulent past was about to catch up with me.

The letter arrived by mail coach, and was, I admit, something of a surprise. As soon as the contents were revealed, the servants took up in a state of unprecedented expectation. Careful not to add to the furore, I kept my own reactions to a minimum. And yet the carnival air was understandable. We don't tend to get many visitors here at Wooten Hall, so the arrival of even the most humble of guests causes something of a stir among the inhabitants. But on this occasion, even I had to sit up straight. For the author of the letter was none other than the Countess of Warwickshire – who also happens to be my bold and enterprising elder sister Elizabeth!

Far from being a timid person by nature, the thought of this rather intimidating creature alighting from her carriage outside my window, did threaten to disturb my composure somewhat. The last time we met was at a ball at Almack's. I was a little worse for wear, having just returned from Rome with Lord Byron. Elizabeth confined her disapproval to a few choice looks, flashed at me from the arms of the cavalry officer she'd engaged during the waltzes. I found her behaviour rather amusing at the time and thought nothing more of it. But like many incidences in life that we dismiss as inconsequential, they often return to haunt us.

Since her marriage to the Earl, a gentleman of high standing and considerable wealth, she had become somewhat remote – at least to me, her troublesome younger brother. I knew not how to address her, nor in which manner, lest this give rise to offence. Suffice to say, that her reputation for propriety and moral rectitude left me suitably distanced; having said that, anyone who can insult the Duchess of Cambridge to her face deserves admiration of some sort! Elizabeth certainly had *bienséance*, as the saying goes, and refused to suffer fools in any capacity.

Preparations began as soon as the ink dried on the paper, and my response to her letter was underway. I called in George, who understood something of the challenge, and instructed him as to the details. Being my oldest and most trusted member of staff, he had about him the inscrutable demeanour of the serving classes, whose facial expressions never once gives them away. His devotion to me was without question. However, I felt it necessary to emphasise the need for discretion in the matter of Elizabeth's visit – especially concerning the recent sale of certain 'valuables', a matter of which I was anxious to keep hidden.

'No doubt, my sister will wish to see the rooms,' I said. 'But on no account is she to visit the Long Gallery. You may invent some pretence that workmen are carrying out renovation and must not be disturbed.'

'Very well, sir.'

'Inform the staff that the lady Elizabeth is to be extended every courtesy, except the freedom of movement beyond the library. It may in fact be prudent to have the entire area cordoned off.'

'I will see to it that your wishes are carried out.'

'And one more thing.'

He stopped at the door, and looked back.

Yes, sir?'

'I take it you've told no one else of this regrettable business?'

'I have honoured your request for discretion, sir.'

Did I detect a note of insolence there? I couldn't be sure. My faith in George's authority wavered a little. Perhaps he was too old to take part in a deception of this kind, and would not be able to contain the staff, whose love for gossip and scandal outweighed any sense of loyalty they might have. All the same, I had little choice. If Elizabeth was to stay, I needed an ally. And more than anyone else, George understood what was at stake. The entire future of Wooten Hall depended upon his discretion.

Filled with a sense of impending dread, I paced the rooms of the upper floors, gazing wistfully at the portraits of my ancestors and reflecting on my less than salubrious past. What would they make of my nocturnal wanderings, my torrid affairs and the casual disregard I'd displayed for my future? Would they gasp in horror at the depths to which I'd descended, and the company I'd kept? God knows, I've tried for the sake of decency to maintain a civilised front, but my reputation always arrives before me, laying the grounds for controversy without me needing to utter a single word.

Indiscretions are an unavoidable pitfall in this world, a lesson so amply demonstrated by my father during his lifetime, despite his repeated attempts to cover them up. But mine have been sobering and 'educational', to say the least. The most recent cloud on the horizon has been one I bitterly regret. Had I been able to avoid the decision I was forced to make, I would've done. But due to the circumstances, and the potential for scandal the incident would've produced, I felt I had no choice. Elizabeth's letter had arrived like some awful portent of reckoning, her imminent arrival arranged deliberately to hold me to account.

Several weeks passed after the receipt of the letter. Then one day, the beat of horses' hooves rang out on the courtyard and the familiar grinding of carriage wheels that signified a visitor. With a mounting sense of trepidation, I went to the window and looked out. There beneath me, assisted by her lady-in-waiting and my stalwart attendant, George, and watched by the entire household staff, was my one and only remaining sibling. The Countess Elizabeth.

Gazing down from my window, a web of conflicting feelings enveloped me. In truth, the lady vexed my spirit in ways I hadn't previously imagined. Her marriage to the Earl had given her a somewhat regal disposition, encouraged, no doubt, by the fortune she'd married into. The death of the Earl's first wife to consumption had left him bereft, and with the added burden of a ten-year-old son. His marriage to Elizabeth seemed to revitalise his spirits, although in the following years their union proved to be childless.

Stepping down from her sumptuous carriage, the like of which one rarely saw on village streets and country lanes, Elizabeth turned to look up at the house. Her face lent itself to a kind of brooding severity, the contours of which, whilst not unattractive, were sharp, even in repose. I saw in her, the disapproving and phlegmatic nature of our late father, whose ruthlessness in business matters was well known.

The very able Mrs Peacock hurried across to lend a supporting arm to Elizabeth's gait. The two were joined, albeit briefly, in an awkward shuffle across the pavers, where they were greeted by a contingent of household staff, who could barely contain their delight. The driver of the carriage also alighted, and handed the reins to a porter, before being ushered over to the servants' quarters for a well-earned rest and bite to eat.

I stayed at the window for some time, gazing out across the old stone wall to the countryside beyond. Both Elizabeth's arrival and the reason behind it were a mystery, alluded to only vaguely in her letter. I suspected that common intrigue might be behind it, given my recent return from Rome, and the controversy surrounding it. The clucking hens who frequented the balls and the grace-and-favour apartments of London would have delighted in the tales of my dissipation, only too keen to pass these rumours along to anyone who cared to listen. But there may've been other reasons for her visit, things I would much rather not think about.

And so the mood changed at Wooten Hall, the staff galvanised into paroxysms of activity. From my upstairs retreat, I could hear the urgent voices and hurried shuffling of feet across the tiled floor. Back from their hunt with the gamekeeper, the dogs barked outside, caught up it would seem by the tumultuous atmosphere. George's voice rang out along the passageways, issuing commands to his underlings with a note of frustration, as if the occasion had disturbed even his unflappable nature.

Overcome with a sense of unease, I remained where I was, counting down the moments where I should be obliged to go down and confront her.

George appeared, his expression composed, as if the recent upheaval hadn't happened.

'The Lady Elizabeth wishes to see you, sir.'

'Of course. I shall be down in a minute.'

'And should I instruct the cook to prepare dinner?'

'Yes, you may. And be sure to use the best porcelain.'

'I believe you sold the Sèvres, sir?'

'Then use the Wedgewood, dammit!'

A moment's awkwardness persisted, during which George observed me with an odd cautionary gaze. Unable to discern its meaning, I chose to dismiss him forthwith, left alone once more to contemplate my sister's appearance. But the strangest feeling remained. When one has behaved deplorably, abandoning all measures of restraint, the long shadows of the past often reach out with icy fingers. Time is a strange thing. It permits one to absorb one's previous transgressions and to reflect upon them with greater clarity. My life up until then had been one of wealth and privilege. I'd travelled a great deal, and mixed with the best in society. No one could accuse me of reticence in any of my affairs. And yet, a serious blight had dimmed the light of my recollections, causing in me a rare weariness of spirit. Instead of the draught of life, I drank of its sorrows and complexities, the little moral conundrums I'd previously dismissed as being beneath my contempt.

My thoughts were interrupted by voices downstairs.

Gripped by a sudden urgency, I slipped on my best dinner jacket, adjusted my lightly starched cravat in the glass, and headed downstairs. Thankfully, the hall was clear, suffused with a pale sunlight that warmed the stone floor. As I crept through in my favourite Turkish slippers, I felt like a foil in one of Shakespeare's plays. Passing through to the drawing room unobserved, I settled into the high-backed chair by the window, there to await my confessor.

'The Countess Elizabeth, sir.'

George's solemn announcement unsettled me. Sitting up with a start, I turned to behold my sister. She stood in the doorway, her figure somewhat muted in the poor light, the paleness of her neckline enhanced by her powder blue muslin dress; her fetching straw bonnet and long kid gloves gave her an elegant look, in keeping with her station. For a moment, it seemed she might stay where she was, prevented from entering by some inexplicable force.

'Do come in,' I said, with as much enthusiasm as I could muster. With that, she stiffened her carriage, and with all the grace nobility had bequeathed her, strode into the drawing room to greet me.

It is somewhat embarrassing for me to recall my reaction that day. I, who have dined with kings and foreign ambassadors, unable to utter even a token gesture. For the first time in my life I'd been bested, struck dumb by the sight of my own sister!

Anointed by the sharp scent of her perfume, I made a formal bow. Our eyes met on a level plain; her height affording me no advantage. But it was her physical appearance that struck me most of all. Where before there had been a certain roundness of form, a hint of corpulence in the jowls and the chin, now there was a distinct reduction. Her youth, it would seem, had given way to an austere and dignified adulthood. I could only admire her current look, and her taste in clothing which accentuated the whole affair.

From here began the formalities, to which we were both well-acquainted.

'How was your journey?' I said.

'Bothersome. The roads are in a dreadful condition.'

'Apparently they're experimenting with a new type of carriage which has a much better suspension. The Regent himself has expressed an interest.'

'Really. Perhaps you could order one for my return journey, then.'

I'd almost forgotten her humour, delivered with the same acute severity, her gaze fixed implacably on mine. And yet, the trace of a long-forgotten affinity stirred between us. Fond childhood recollections that bound us together, in spite of our many differences.

'Please, take a seat,' I said, with feigned hospitality. 'I'll ring George for some refreshment.'

Lowering herself cautiously into the armchair, she adjusted herself to the new position and folded her hands demurely in her lap. I took the chair several feet away, and prepared myself for the ordeal which would surely follow. Here we were, the two of us, alone in the old house that contained so many memories, and neither one of us entirely prepared for what might happen next.

With her gaze once more settled upon me, she sniffed abruptly and deigned to speak. 'You know why I've come, of course?'

'To enquire after my health, I assume?'

Ignoring my attempt at humour, she continued in the same vein. 'I feel I must broach a difficult subject, Henry. Had I been able to spare you the indignity I most certainly would.'

'Well, I'm sure that whatever it is can wait until after dinner.'

'You always did have a gift for levity, didn't you?' She looked away, her imperious gaze taking in the wood panelling and the family portraits. In different circumstances I might have found her candour refreshing; she had a way of confronting delicate issues without the circumnavigation so beloved of our social circles. On this occasion, however, I lacked the resources to do battle, and sought the coward's retreat.

Without warning, she shot me a piercing look.

'Is it true what they say in London?'

'I'm sure they say many things.'

'Don't be clever with me, Henry, it doesn't become you ... I'm talking about the debts you've run up. The foreclosure on the apartment at St James's.'

I met her gaze with some difficulty, pondering my own somewhat inadequate position. It was true, I had squandered a fortune with my aimless wandering, travelling from London to Rome, accompanying Lord Byron – with whom I shared several memorable excursions. My love of the bookmakers and the dice, which, unfortunately, consumed much of my income, along with the small fortune spent on my attire. I believed wholeheartedly in the old dictum, that a gentleman should dress in the style befitting his status, regardless of his immediate circumstances.

'As you may be aware,' I said. 'I incurred some rather unfortunate business losses, which resulted in me being unable to keep the apartment in London.'

'I heard a different story, that the whole unfortunate business was due to gambling debts you couldn't pay.'

'Gossip, Elizabeth. These people have nothing better to do with their time.'

She stared at me, puzzled it would appear.

'Do you care nothing for your reputation?'

'On the contrary, my reputation is something I've come to regard with the greatest affection, even if it does tend to ebb and flow like the tide.'

Unimpressed, she sniffed, and tapped her fingernails on the arm of the chair. Afternoon shadows lengthened across the granite floor, clouds forming beyond the window. Elizabeth's countenance took on a sharp, almost baleful appearance, like some harbinger of doom come to disturb my tranquillity. I longed to escape the gloomy atmosphere, to initiate some impromptu gaiety to liven things up.

I rang to summon George; the appearance of an ally might alleviate some of the tension and give me a much needed break. Until then I had to play the role of genial host.

'I believe Mrs Peacock has prepared a room for you in the old wing,' I said. 'With the fire lit you should be more than comfortable.'

'I should like to see the upper rooms before I go.'

I hesitated before replying, caught out by the unexpected request. 'That may not be possible. Did George not say? I've had workmen in to repair some of the crumbling masonry, and it's still not finished.'

'How convenient.'

At this juncture, I chose caution as the best way forward. Had we been pieces on a chessboard, I would have been *en prise* to Elizabeth's relentless attack; my beleaguered pawn to her black knight. But whatever move I made seemed destined to be anticipated by her and blocked accordingly. Her contempt at my past behaviour was underscored by everything she said, an impasse preventing any reasonable discourse between us.

George appeared in the doorway, straight as a musket, white gloved hands at his side. His face revealed nothing, trained as it was from decades of servitude.

'You rang, sir?'

'Would you bring refreshments, George? I'm sure Elizabeth is thirsty after such a long journey.'

'Of course ... And may I say what a privilege it is to have my lady stay at Wooten Hall.'

Elizabeth accepted his platitude with a gracious nod of her head, and watched his departure with interest. I observed their brief interaction with curiosity – especially Elizabeth's response. This studied arrangement of mouth and limb that brooked no opposition. And me, her younger brother, forced to sit there and take it like a bankrupt hussar.

George left, and we were alone again. By now, my anxiety had risen accordingly. Her request to see the upper floors had thrown me into confusion. Herein lay perhaps my greatest fear, that my single act of desperation several weeks previously should be discovered, and broadcast the length and breadth of the land. This house, with its Norman origins and Tudor gardens, host to a long line of royals and archdukes, which had passed over to me when my father died. To have inherited such a monument has been both a curse and a blessing, forcing me to abandon a life devoted singularly to pleasure for one of duty and responsibility. But my deception would have grave repercussions if found out.

I tried another tack, this time to draw Elizabeth into less contentious territory.

'How's Robert?' I said. 'Is he still thinking of joining the Prince of Wales' Own?'

'Robert will stay on at Eton until he comes of age, then he'll discuss the various options open to him with his father.'

'I'm sure he'll look rather splendid in uniform. And Eton, of course, will prepare him more than adequately for the wider world.'

'As it prepared you, no doubt.'

I recalled my own innings at that eminent school, catching rats in the old building, and fighting with locals by the river; a welcome release from the rigours of Greek and Latin. There we gave 'humble and hearty thanks' for Henry VI, our illustrious founder, whose rather diffident portrait watched over us in the main hall. It was during that time that I had my first serious liaison with a local girl called Kitty Drake, who instructed me in the arts of pleasing a lady. I can still recall her beckoning finger and wicked gaze, summoning me to her inner chamber. Her plump and yielding flesh, that to a naïve schoolboy was like a lush and undiscovered continent.

George came in with the refreshments, his entrance giving me time to reassess. He stopped the trolley between us, and poured a measure of wine. Thankfully, Elizabeth accepted, with a curt nod of her head, and sat glass in hand, waiting for us to be alone again.

'Will that be all, sir?'

'That'll be all, thank you.'

With a formal bow, George turned to leave, and once again I noted a brief but unmistakable look of collusion pass between him and Elizabeth. I tried to put it out of my mind, to dismiss it as inconsequential, but it remained on the periphery, contributing to my burden of doubt.

Once again, Elizabeth and I faced each other across the divide, like contestants in a parlour game. Perhaps we should have donned masks and engaged in a proper little masquerade, our real identities hidden. But such a quaint *pas de deux* could never be. I, who once bore the dubious distinction of being blackballed from White's – after spending a fortune at the dice tables, I might add! Elizabeth, of course, indulged in the more respectable pursuits, like horse-riding and playing the piano, and wouldn't be seen dead in the type of places I frequented.

'I hope the wine is to your liking,' I said. 'I had it shipped in from Bordeaux.'

'At a considerable cost, I'm sure.'

'One cannot put too high a price on good-living. Isn't that what Father used to say?'

'He also said that a man should never live beyond his means, advice you've clearly never taken.'

In a strange way, Elizabeth reminded me of the Contessa Francesca of Milan, whose volcanic eruptions were legendary. And yet, being somewhat resourceful in this area, I pursued her with a singleness of purpose, until, quite dramatically one evening, she gave in. Something of a connoisseur by then, I understood the nuances, the toing and froing that goes on between a hound and his quarry. But where Francesca hid a passionate and eager heart behind her initial reticence, Elizabeth's was purely glacial. As my older sister, she was fully aware of my little habits, my *manières de se comporter*, as the French might say, and disapproved of them vigorously.

And so, with my dubious past once again under scrutiny, I began to feel a keen sense of melancholy. My youth had gone, lost in foreign cities and exotic climes. The jewel that had glittered briefly in the gentlemen's clubs and the dance halls of Europe, illuminating the faces of those caught in its embrace, had left me destitute and without prospects. I now had to consider a future without its thrall, alone in my late father's house, suffering the first stirrings of ill-health, the consequences of which I could scarcely consider.

'What happened to Emily?'

The name struck me like the shot from a cannon, leaving me momentarily stunned. In all of Elizabeth's accusations, none had ventured into this most personal territory thus far.

I recovered enough to proffer an answer.

'I dismissed her. She'd become ... troublesome.'

'You mean, she was pregnant.' Elizabeth watched me with a shrewd and accusatory gaze. I couldn't help my increasing bewilderment.

'How the devil did you come by that information?'

'Word travels, Henry. Even *you* must have thought of that.'

Now I had another dilemma. Not only did Elizabeth know of the circumstances surrounding Emily's departure, but I had to try and explain without implicating myself further.

'I'm surprised that the fortunes of a mere serving girl should warrant so much attention,' I said. 'As I understand it, she found employment with a family in Reigate.'

'The same family you paid fifty-pounds to secure her position and keep the whole thing quiet?'

How I wished for a carriage to hurry me away to some other part of the country to escape her stinging barbs. This relentless determination of hers to expose my shortcomings that had led us to an impasse so early on in our conversation. What could I say in my defence? A man's appetites are many and varied, and depending on his inclinations can be indulged in a variety of ways. Having been somewhat overenthusiastic in my youth, I enjoyed the ladies' company perhaps a little too much – such liaisons interrupting my studies and almost preventing my late entry to the bar. I also found these alluring creatures to be far better companions than many of my male friends, whose coarseness and vulgarity often bored me to distraction.

Emily had all the attributes of the perfect companion. Dark in complexion, with lustrous eyes to match, I could talk to her about any subject at all, and she would lie in my arms and listen, always with that rapt look so common to the lower orders. Somewhat passive in repose, she did, however, possess a certain willingness for congress that fair quickens the pulse and fires the blood. Her body I came to know as intimately as the law books in my father's library, and spent many an hour exploring every line and contour of its delightful proximity.

'The entire business was regrettable,' I said. 'I became rather more involved than I'd intended.'

'Yes, I'm sure. You'd have found a far better transaction at King's Place, and saved yourself the trouble.'

Her reference to this rather infamous area of London surprised me. And yet it was true, I had regularly frequented such establishments, enjoying the company of the industrious girls who plied their trade there. Then, in more upmarket settings, the acquaintance of such celebrated courtesans as Julia Johnstone and Harriette Wilson.

However, I detected something other than mere censure in Elizabeth's reaction. The way she avoided my gaze, and the distinctly uncomfortable look in her eyes. It puzzled me, but I couldn't quite decipher the cause.

'You're wrong about Emily,' I said.

'Why?'

'Because she was good for me. I loved her – more than any woman I've ever known.'

The silence enveloped us both. I'd said far more than I intended, but the few words I had said carried the incontrovertible ring of truth.

Tired of my wistful reminiscence, Elizabeth leaned forward, focused and hawk-like.

'I really couldn't care less about this *serving girl*, as you put it. But I will not sit here and have you lie to me. I take it you got rid of her to avoid the embarrassment?'

'I could not be certain the child was mine.'

'And that's your defence, is it? Consorting with a domestic and then sending her away to avoid taking any responsibility for the consequences?'

'I was going through a rather difficult time.'

'Excuses! that's all I've ever heard from you. Even when Father was alive you couldn't help but blame whatever misfortune you'd encountered on somebody else. Never once did you stop to think of the shame you might bring on yourself, and on your family.'

It was at that moment that I understood. The bitterness in her voice. Her refusal to empathise with my predicament. Her marriage to the Earl had, up until now, been childless. My seemingly casual disregard for a pregnant serving girl must have offended her deeply.

She sniffed imperiously, and shifted her position in the chair. 'You should have bought a commission like Stephen. A foreign campaign might have kept you out of trouble.'

'I never cared much for the army – and neither does Wellington by all accounts. My good friend Harcott is a Lieutenant-Colonel on the Peninsula, and according to him, good officers are thin on the ground.'

'Yes, I'm sure that's true,' she said, agreeing with me for the first time. 'Stephen says the French have become an undisciplined rabble. The spoils of war, it seems, are the ruination of good soldiering. Men march better on an empty stomach than on one filled with port and brandy.'

How madam had been influenced by her husband, whose military aphorisms had crept into her vocabulary like assassins in an enemy camp. Suffice to say, he and I never got on. This profligate brother-in-law of his who sought comfort over sacrifice, and preferred the soirees of high society to a grim death on the battlefield. But at least we'd moved away from the discomfiting subject of Emily.

Elizabeth sipped her wine, her gaze hovering somewhere above my head. 'All that wandering you did,' she said. 'Where did it get you? Why didn't you take a wife and settle down?'

'I should certainly have liked to, had the opportunity arisen. But one can't look back and change things, can one?'

When a gentleman looks for qualities in a prospective match, he has to consider many different factors, not least of these being the lineage of the girl in question. My father wanted me to marry the Lady Jane, daughter of the Duke of Gloucester, but I had other ideas. This brief and rather unfortunate acquaintance soon made way for the aforementioned Contessa Francesca of Milan, whose unpredictable and explosive temperament often made it dangerous for me to remain in her company for too long. Then there were the regular trawls through the bars and the bordellos, where the niceties of society life were non-existent. Here, I found a peculiar kind of solace among those who shared my interests. But the eyes of love are hungry and gorge themselves until they're full. One tends to leave these places with more than one had bargained for, the soul a little more tainted.

Weary of our little debate, I felt the need for a change of setting. 'How about a stroll in the garden before dinner?' I said. 'You can tell me all about Stephen's escapades in France.'

And so to the garden we went, with its roses and carnations, cotton lavender and golden marjoram, its ornate paths that divided the neat squares of lawn. Looking back at the grey stone of the house and its latticed windows, I was seized by a tremendous sadness. The futility of my previous existence had brought me to this, a defeat as catastrophic as any Wellington might have endured. And Wooten Hall with its limestone walls and crenelated rooftops, the grand sense of majesty that imposed itself upon awestruck visitors. Was I really destined to forego its rustic charms and accept defeat?

Elizabeth gazed out over the garden, perhaps with the same regret. The first time she'd been here in years, the place of her birth and upbringing. We may have had a difference in temperament, but like the lichen that grew beneath the mullion windows, our past was entwined here irrevocably. This house, which had been in the family since the original owners had abandoned it in the twelfth century; since then, it had undergone many refurbishments, inside and out, not least the Tudor garden and the Long Gallery, designed and inaugurated by the indomitable Bess of Shrewsbury. And the secret that I'd kept from her so diligently, having entrusted the details to George, threatened to be the end of me completely.

Stopping by the hedgerow, she looked out over the neighbouring meadows.

'I used to ride out there for hours,' she said. 'Father used to say that if anything happened to me no one would ever know.'

'Yes, and what an expert you were. You could've led the Scots Greys.'

With a disdainful little sniff, she turned back to the house. For one heart-stopping moment, I imagined I saw Emily standing at one of the windows looking out. I had to blink rapidly to dispel the illusion.

'What's the matter?' Elizabeth said, noting my distress.

'Nothing, I was just admiring the view.'

The vision faded, but the image remained, troubling in its persistence.

I felt unusually cold, a condition which has troubled me on and off these past few weeks; this, coupled with the aching joints that plague me at night. As a result, I must admit to being uncharacteristically irate a good deal of the time, a mood I'm sure even the servants noticed. But I had to maintain this grand façade, at least until the whole thing was over and Elizabeth was safely on her way home.

'Shall we head back?' I said, assuming my gallant demeanour. Inwardly, I prepared for the next unexpected attack. So far, our conversation had skirted the borders, like a dance where the participants hang back waiting for a suitable opportunity to engage. But if I was eager to find out exactly *why* Elizabeth had come to visit, I wasn't to be kept waiting long.

On the way back to the house, she became unusually quiet. I could almost sense the doubt and recriminations turning over in that pretty little head.

'I've arranged for us to dine in the main hall,' I said. 'I believe the cook has prepared a marvellous side of beef he procured from the market.'

'I hope you haven't gone to too much trouble on my behalf. After all, I didn't come here to be entertained.'

'But one expects a certain standard of hospitality from one's host, as I'm sure you would agree.'

'You don't have to butter me up, Henry.'

By now I was becoming restless, her mood leading me to several wild conclusions. Perhaps her society friends had supplied her with more than just gossip, and I was about to be exposed for an even greater indiscretion. To cover one's tracks, one must be adept in all manner of deception – and to be able to recall in the minutest detail the lies one has told whenever certain subjects come up. But I'd become increasingly careless over the years, leaving me open to all manner of charges.

We stood in the courtyard, where she drank in a draught of the late-afternoon air. The weight of so much uncertainty had me in its grip. Finally, I could stand her silence no longer.

'Is something troubling you, Elizabeth?'

She turned to me, and without the slightest urgency, said, 'Perhaps we could go inside. I should like to dress before dinner.'

Relieved somewhat, I took to my room on the upper floor, gaining respite from this most awkward of circumstances. Easing off my boots, I lay back upon the bed, and pondered this seemingly intractable problem. Technically speaking, I was destitute. My accountant had reckoned up the sum of my assets and pronounced them inadequate to my needs. My creditors had all applied to the high court for restitution, hence the sale of the apartment at St James's to pay off some of my debts. The life I had lived before – one of 'gay abandon', as my good friend Harcott would say – was little more than a lurid memory. Having inherited a considerable fortune, and of course my father's good name, I chose to ignore the wiser precepts of business and embraced a style of living that many would call reckless. Not only that, but as a consequence of my adventures at home and abroad, I had acquired something the French referred to as *le grande verole*. I was, to put it mildly, in a bit of a fix.

At the appointed hour, I dressed in my finest attire, adjusted my cravat, and spent a few moments admiring the effect in the mirror. It has been a feature of my recent misfortune, that I've been unable to gaze upon my reflection with anything other than disdain. The clothes that hang in my wardrobe, once a matter of pride and satisfaction, now seem to highlight my personal failings as if they were made for this purpose alone. And yet, still, I couldn't help a cautious vanity, that here in the velvet seams of my disgraced countenance were the embers of a fire that had once blazed throughout Europe, capturing the hearts of countesses and courtesans alike.

The wooden beams of the Great Hall loomed over us as we took our places at the dining table, Elizabeth at one end, myself at the other. On one wall, the tapestry depicting a hunt, a mixture of nobles on horseback and the peasant contingent on foot – complete with their shiny red faces and drab costumes. As a child, the scene used to fascinate me, especially the distress on the face of the wild boar, speared by a lance. Even then, my innate sensitivity and aversion to bloodshed precluded the military career my father had planned for me.

George brought the wine, and proceeded to pour, first for madam, and then, with the same inscrutable deliberation, for my good self. Stepping back, he awaited further instruction.

'Thank you, George. That'll be all.'

With a formal bow, he turned and marched out. I looked for the same conspiratorial glance he'd shared with Elizabeth earlier, but whatever it may have alluded to remained hidden.

Dinner arrived, brought in on the best Wedgewood by a train of servants who hovered silently and respectfully behind us as we began. And so we ate, the two of us, at the fine polished walnut table that had been among the family's possessions since the reign of Queen Anne. I thought, ruefully, how all this finery would soon be denied me, that I would be confined to my room on meagre rations. The hopes I had entertained, the aspirations I still had left, would never be realised – a cruel trick of nature, that it reworks one's dreams and turns them into something far less palatable.

Elizabeth put down her knife and fork, and allowed her food to digest, all the while maintaining her outer composure.

'Were you really in love with her?' she said.

For a moment, I was confused. The question had the makings of another trap, in which to implicate me further.

'With whom?'

'Oh come on, Henry. Whom do you think I mean? ... That *girl* – Emily.'

The flesh is a marvellous piece of work, and has never failed to elicit a favourable response in me whenever I've sampled its delights. But one can have too much of a good thing, as I came to realise. Emily loved me unconditionally. She never once spoke of these feelings, but it was there in her gaze, and the way she clung to me during the heights of our lovemaking. The hardest thing I ever had to do was send her away. Her absence left a huge hole in my heart and blackened my days for months on end.

'She was a distraction,' I lied. 'Had I more sense, I should have never have become involved.'

'It was Father's wish that you marry Lady Jane. Why didn't you?'

'Because, quite frankly, she was boring. Had I married her I would've ended up throwing myself from the ramparts in a fit of pique.'

'And yet such a union might've produced an heir. You would not be in the position you now find yourself in.'

'True. But I would also have been beholden to her father, whose view of me wasn't exactly favourable at the best of times.'

Elizabeth pondered, dabbing her mouth with a napkin. I couldn't help but review the previous decades, the expectations put upon me from an early age to behave in a certain way. Marriage to Lady Jane would have been of huge import to my father, who saw it as a step up in the social hierarchy, and more or less guaranteed financial remuneration. But he underestimated the spirit of rebellion within me, perhaps inherited from my mother, God rest her, whose own claims to independence were fiercely defended throughout her relatively short life. Perhaps because of her influence, I gravitated towards strong women, who tended to speak freely and candidly, even at risk to their person. Lady Jane was outwardly meek and docile, willing to do her father's bidding in all her affairs unquestioningly. I saw something in her that I didn't particularly like – and she, with a keen perception even I had to acknowledge, understood that marrying me would hardly bring the contentment she was seeking.

The serving girls cleared away the dishes, making sure to keep their gaze from the incumbents at either end of the table. As they left, Elizabeth gave a little cough, to remind me that we had yet to close our little discussion.

'Did you enjoy the meal?' I said.

'Yes, thank you.'

'Would you like to go to your room now?'

'Please don't hurry me, Henry, you'll give me an indigestion.'

Madam's wit has always been as sharp as a sabre, keen to thrust and parry with the best of them. Tonight she seemed a trifle lacklustre, not quite herself in many ways. Perhaps she'd grown tired of criticising me, and wished because of my dire circumstances to offer a balm to aid me. But in keeping with the protocol I'd been observing my entire life, I showed not a flicker of apprehension.

'I'm truly sorry that I've put you to all this trouble, Elizabeth. It was never my intention to embarrass or humiliate you in any way.'

'Your contrition doesn't become you. I'd much rather you were honest with me and didn't hide behind platitudes.'

'Well, I don't deny that my actions have been a little ... impulsive, shall we say. But that's the nature of business, as you're well aware. Fortunes tend to go one way and then the other, and sometimes all one can do is sit on the side-lines and observe.'

'That's why you sold the paintings, is it?'

I froze, completely taken aback. The question called for a response I wasn't immediately able to give.

Elizabeth observed me carefully from the other end of the table, her gaze beguilingly neutral. 'Did you really think you could get away with something on that scale without anyone finding out?'

I sank back in the chair, the half-filled glass of wine in front of me. Now, in the light of such an unexpected revelation, I had to decide how to conduct my own defence. Several questions turned over in my head. How much did Elizabeth know, and who was her source? And, most importantly, how the devil could I talk my way out of it without digging an even deeper hole?

'I had to take certain steps to meet my obligations,' I said. 'As I've already explained, sale of the apartment in London wasn't enough to square my debts. Then, of course, I've had the upkeep of Wooten Hall. The maintenance. The servants. All these things have been a tremendous drain on my resources.'

'So you simply sold off paintings that'd been in the family for several centuries without telling anyone? Without even bothering to ask me?'

'Three portraits and a landscape, to be precise.'

'And the Vermeer?'

'Unfortunately, yes. I had no choice.'

She shook her head, her eyes never leaving mine. 'I wish I could find some sympathy for you. How easy do you think it's been for me, forced to listen to tales of your wantoness and being unable to defend you. Why didn't you come to me? Have I really been so unapproachable?'

I hung my head in a parody of shame, buying myself a valuable few seconds. The candles on the table flickered in sympathy, casting us both in a melancholy light.

'Were you going to tell me what you'd done?'

'Of course. In fact, it was my sincere intention to buy the paintings back whenever I was able.'

She laughed abruptly, a sharp retort that echoed in the room. 'You really did miss your vocation, didn't you? You should've been on the stage with David Garrick, and we could've all paid to see you perform.'

Under different circumstances I might have imagined a note of admiration in her tone. I was used to confrontations of this kind, having extricated myself from similar spots on many occasions. However, this was indeed a tough blow to parry. Even as severe a critic as Elizabeth could not pierce the cool exterior I'd built up over several decades as a student of diplomacy. From my schooldays at Eton, to my entry into high society as a young lord, I'd established what the dons called 'character.' But now this mask had been torn from me, revealing my true face.

The time had come to end our little dispute over material things. I was going to wait until after dinner, but a sense of urgency made it seem appropriate to speak now. The subject matter was not at all to my liking, and most certainly would not be to hers, but it had to be confronted. I could no longer live with the shame.

'I have something else to tell you,' I said. 'Something rather delicate, unfortunately.'

'Please don't tell me you've sold the house?'

Now madam was finding a little humour of her own. Sadly, I could find nothing to raise my own spirits, and proceeded with a heavy heart.

'I paid a visit to Dr Morton in London recently. He specialises in certain ... diseases.'

Her curiosity aroused, she drew herself up in the chair, preparing herself for whatever shock I might deliver.

'It appears as if my frequent travels abroad have resulted in me acquiring a certain ... inconvenience, shall we say.'

'Scarlet fever?'

'Not quite.'

It is, of course, the most natural thing in the world for a man to indulge his passions. And I, for one, have been most fortunate in the opportunities presented me during my odyssey around the globe. But aside from the physical pleasures, my memories have always been of the companionship and the romance, the endless promise of those who have fallen for my advances and reciprocated enthusiastically. Whenever luck has deserted me – which it has done on many occasions – I have invariably been rescued by a woman, who has through her own administrations restored me to a semblance of vigour. I could not have imagined a life without such sublime pleasures. Tragically, this was the prospect I now faced.

'I never imagined my life would end this way,' I said. 'Reduced to the status of a destitute. Those who'd once made such efforts to secure my company, now doing their best to look the other way.'

'What on earth are you talking about?'

But of course I couldn't tell her. To do so would have upset her refined sensibilities and ruined my reputation completely. They call it the French disease. Dr Morton says I probably picked it up in a brothel; such places are breeding grounds for this particular complaint. But now I faced the grim realisation that the symptoms had come back after lying dormant for so long. In short, I could only allude to the diagnosis, and hope that Elizabeth would find it within herself to see me in a more compassionate light.

'Let's just say that I'm paying the price for a former indulgence,' I said. 'The carousel ride I've been on for some considerable time is finally over.'

Her expression shifted, almost imperceptibly – a subtle withdrawal of the animosity she'd accorded me earlier. Encouraged by her change in demeanour, I continued in a similar vein, being as honest as I possibly could under the circumstances.

'There is, as far as I'm aware, no cure. Unless one considers the sweat baths and the mercury treatment, which Dr Morton thinks are a temporary measure at best.'

'What will you do?'

'What options are left to me? I have no money, no prospects.'

'And whose fault is that but your own?'

Brought up by the sudden coldness in her tone, I shook my head in a kind of bemused admiration. 'Is there anything in my current situation that moves you at all?'

'I came here with the express intention of saving you from further disgrace, but I see now that my intentions were misguided. You've brought this calamity upon yourself, and nothing I do or say can change it.'

How the differences between us were highlighted right there at the dining table in the flickering candlelight. Elizabeth in her pale blue muslin dress and matching jacket, her gaze trained upon me like an elegant bird of prey. Myself, a victim of cruel circumstance, dressed impeccably in the most fashionable garb, and yet unable to afford even the price of a cheap cigar. And how, through the long years of separation, we had taken markedly different courses, which had altered our lives irrevocably and driven us even further apart.

Something else troubled me. The intimation that, in spite of her apparent candour, Elizabeth was not yet finished.

'You came to see me of your own volition,' I said, 'knowing that to do so would cause further speculation among your pious friends. What would they think of you now, sitting here drinking wine with a bankrupt, a man who has parted company with his former reputation, and been handed a death sentence to boot?'

'You're still my brother.'

'Reason enough to proffer charity, it would seem.'

'What would you rather – debtor's prison? She shifted in the chair, the layers of her frock sighing in response. Her gaze fell upon the wood panelling, the tapestry, as if seeing it for the first time.

'Stephen thinks we should requisition the house,' she said.

'The house?'

'Surely you didn't think you could hang on to it?'

'I'm sorry?'

She wiped her mouth with a napkin, in no hurry to explain. 'I can't decide whether you think me stupid or simply ill-informed. Did it not occur to you that I would make my own enquiries?'

'At the risk of appearing a little backward – into what, may I ask?'

'I went to London at the suggestion of my solicitor, and asked a high court judge to make your financial records available for inspection.'

'You did what!'

'You left me no choice. I had to do what I thought was necessary.'

After the shock had worn off, I couldn't help a begrudging admiration. I pictured Elizabeth, in her stately garb, bending to inspect a ledger filled with evidence of my serial derelictions. For some obscure reason the thought amused me.

Her eyes bored into mine, always on the lookout for any perceived irreverence.

'I'm glad you think it so funny,' she said. 'Something you'd like to share with me?'

'Pardon my ignorance, Elizabeth, but why on earth would you go to such lengths to examine my finances? Why didn't you simply ask me?'

'Because I wouldn't have got the truth.' Struck, perhaps, by a measure of sympathy, her hard countenance wavered. She softened her tone. 'I'm sorry, Henry. You've left me no choice but to intercede. My solicitors are all set to make the necessary changes.'

'Changes?'

'Father made certain stipulations in the will. In the event of neglect, or in matters of bankruptcy, ownership of the house would revert to the oldest surviving sibling – which in this instance is me.'

I felt the stirrings of an irrational resentment, at Elizabeth, her solicitors and the high court judge, whose ruling would open me up to all manner of humiliation. Then, of course, at my own father for making such a heartless provision in the first place.

'And what does the *Earl* make of it all?' I said, using his title with a derogatory flourish. 'Will he too join my creditors to watch me swing from the gallows?'

Elizabeth responded with scorn, a concentration of all the forces she might use against me. '*Stephen* has always supported me in everything I do. And, I might remind you how generous he was when you needed assistance in Milan. One more episode that brought shame on the family, and proved how utterly irresponsible you are.'

Even I had to admit how impressed I was with the way the affair was handled. The Earl always did have impeccable standards – not to mention his contacts abroad, which saved me from the likelihood of incarceration in a foreign prison.

'Oh well,' I said flippantly. 'What is life but a rich pageant from which we can all gain an education.'

Elizabeth shook her head with distaste. 'Even now, given the humiliating position you're in, you can't resist making a jest out of the situation, can you?'

'On the contrary, I'm merely making light of it so as not to spoil dessert. The cook makes a wonderful pistachio.'

I made no attempt to feign surprise. In fact, the thought had occurred to me once or twice before, when I'd weighed up the various possibilities.

'Have you nothing else to say?'

I shrugged, worn down by the whole sorry business. 'What else *is* there to say? You've outlined the purpose of your visit. Coming here to oust me from my own residence.'

'You make it sound as if I'm being mercenary. Such an

arrangement would, in fact, help ease your current plight.'

'And how could that possibly be?'

'If you weren't so presumptuous you might allow me to explain.'

Sometimes, when all other avenues are closed, and the only course left is to capitulate, there exists a curious resistance in one's very marrow. Especially when all eyes are watching, anticipating your less than dignified exit from centre stage.

Considering the salient points, and my own unfavourable position, I felt very little 'fighting spirit'. Elizabeth had me, like a hare in a trap.

But there was one more murky detail to confront, one that had been perplexing me all evening.

'Before we go any further, I must ask you. Who told you about the paintings?'

'Does it really matter?'

'I'm curious, that's all.'

She peered at me the length of the table, a moment's hesitation as if she were wrestling with a sudden attack of conscience.

'George told me.'

I stared at her dumbfounded.

'*George?*'

'Please don't think ill of him, Henry. He was so concerned by your behaviour he thought it best to inform me right away. People do actually care about you, you know.'

The shock of hearing this latest betrayal rendered me speechless. George, my personal valet of some years, who bagged seats for me at the opera, and accompanied me on trips to Paris and Rome; a man whose discretion in matters of potential embarrassment was a given. Perhaps the hardest lessons in life come from those closest to us, whose actions we least suspect.

Elizabeth took a sip of wine, and regarded me over the rim of her glass. 'Now ... if we could return to the subject of the house?' ...

She talked at length, while I stared mutely at the white flames of the candelabra. I heard only segments, the details of which would all be tied up by Mr Fox, her highly-efficient solicitor in London. For me, the great romance was over. Having lived my life in a style to which I'd become accustomed, there was nothing left to contemplate but a pauper's grave. And if I managed to escape the ignominious experience of debtor's prison – as she so pointedly reminded me - I should still be cast adrift on a sea of troubles with no income and none of the highborn contacts I'd made who'd rescued me on previous occasions.

Having finished her closing speech, Elizabeth sat back to observe me.

'Are you in agreement?'

I took a sip of wine, savouring the taste as if it might be my last. 'If such a thing were to go ahead, I assume you'd want me out right away?'

'Not at all. I've discussed it with Stephen and he thinks it perfectly acceptable that you stay on. You would, of course, continue to occupy the rooms on the upper floor. The rest of the house would be out of bounds to you.'

'I'd be like a prisoner, then – locked up in an ivory tower?'

'Stephen would rent the rest of the house to military friends. This shouldn't cause you any inconvenience, I'm sure.'

I sank further into my chair, the wood panelling and the stained-glass windows now glowing in a kind of dizzying half-light. The house that had been in the family for two centuries or more, about to be turned into a billet for the 10th Hussars. And I, the catalyst for all this turmoil, was to be abandoned to the upper floors, while the officers from Stephen's regiment dined in my absence.

'Think about it,' she said. 'You can give me your answer in the morning.'

What was there to think about? I simply had no other option. Elizabeth, it seemed, had exhausted all she had to say on the subject. All that was left was to get through dinner, which, understandably, I had little stomach for.

She sat back and folded her hands in her lap, observing me with curiosity.

'What was it?'

'I beg your pardon?'

'The child that girl gave birth to. I assume you know that much?'

I thought hard before answering.

'I believe it was a boy.'

We sat with the delicate subject between us. The child I'd never met, which to all intents could well have been mine, in spite of rumours to the contrary. And the childless state of Elizabeth's marriage, which had prompted her earlier outburst.

Perhaps I might've been happy with Emily, had fate not intervened and decided otherwise. Her lightness of spirit and hearty laugh might've raised me from the depths of melancholy, to which I so often succumbed.

It seemed that we would part company like this. I, with my prospects dashed, and Elizabeth with the controlling rights to my immediate future.

And yet, there remained in me a vestige of the slimmest hope. The sunshine on the continent, where I had spent so many idyllic summers, beckoned me with a languorous hand. Surely this would be a fitting postscript to a life of such abandon.

'What if I were to live abroad?' I said.

'How could you possibly do that? You have no means to support you?'

'But since it would be in yours and your husband's name, the house would release a good deal of equity, surely?'

'To pay the debts you've accumulated because of your idle pursuit of pleasure.' She sat up, and straightened her dress with a sharp tug, glaring at me across the candelabra. 'I don't understand you. By your own admission, you've frittered away the fortune you had at your disposal. You've led a wastrel's life, squandering whatever talents you had in order to pursue all manner of empty promises. Now you're asking *me* to fund a trip abroad.'

'One can live as cheaply in Spain as one can anywhere. I'm not expecting to end up in a palace.'

'Thank heavens for that!' Her outburst contained the faintest kernel of amusement, manifested in a crinkling around the eyes and the faint pursing of her lips as she tried to suppress a smile.

Sensing a minor victory, I pressed on.

'I have friends in Madrid who would be only too happy to find me lodgings. I could write them immediately and have a response within a week or so.'

'And what of your health? This ... condition?'

'I can find a doctor who specialises in treatment. The climate will help, too.'

Elizabeth remained silent for a long time, her head bowed in thought. When she looked up, she appeared to have reached some momentous decision.

'I'll speak to Stephen. See what he thinks.'

'I'm sure it will work out for all concerned.'

She eyed me narrowly. 'Please don't think me a fool, Henry. I'm only doing what I think is right and nothing more ... Now, I think I should like to retire, if you don't mind?'

I showed her to her room, and watched from the doorway as she reacquainted herself with the décor. She stood at the window, perhaps picturing her younger self riding across the moor. If she had regrets she would never reveal them. Certainly not to me. Henry Colville II, her reckless and profligate younger brother.

A Study In Madness

Dr Emile Cousteau sat at his desk and opened the file marked 'Maurice Duvall.' The initial document was a report by the prefect of police made shortly after the subject's arrest. The report went on to describe Duvall's general demeanour, and the answers he'd given under interrogation. To his observers he was responsive and engaging throughout, and made no attempt to deny the charges, claiming he had no recollection of his movements at all. On the night in question, he claimed to have woken in his room in an apartment on the Boulevard Haussmann and wandered outside. Arrested by the gendarmes, he was taken to the police station and questioned extensively. His supposed victim, the young English aristocrat, Lord Hamilton, died of gunshot wounds the next day.

The next document was the original assessment of Duvall's mental state, made by the prison doctor a week after his arrest. Clipped to this was a black and white photograph of the subject himself looking a little bleary-eyed, his round, steel-framed spectacles giving him a stern academic look. Otherwise, he was well-dressed and presentable, as befitting a man of his previous good standing. There was, it seemed, a distinct refinement in his features, and a readiness to meet any challenges, a quality that shone from his clear and untroubled gaze.

The prison doctor's report gave Cousteau an insight into Duvall's mind at the time of the murder. Disregarding the lengthy and sometimes lurid details of the crime itself, he looked for clues that might help him make his own assessment. The subject's response to questioning, and the behaviour noted during his incarceration, was of particular interest. When asked about his relationship with the deceased, Duvall replied simply, 'We were acquaintances, that is all.'

Cousteau continued to read, intrigued by the evaluation. 'Duvall exhibits the symptoms of a homicidal monomania, and seems unable to grasp the gravity of the charges made against him, or to acknowledge his own guilt. It is the recommendation of this committee that he continues to undergo further assessment in readiness for his trial, and to be placed under strict observation at all times.'

Beneath the report was a handwritten document, made on several pages of prison notepaper in a neat, cursive style, as if the author had taken considerable pride in its presentation. At the end, it had been signed *Maurice Duvall*, with a rather elegant flourish.

Leaning back in his chair, Cousteau began to read:

It is the burden of the malcontent to feel he was born at the wrong time. Having harboured similar sentiments throughout my life, I have, for the most part, maintained a considerable optimism and joie de vivre, in spite of the many obstacles I've had to overcome. From as early as I can remember, I was alive with all kinds of whimsical ideas and energies. By the age of ten I was drawing detailed sketches of the anatomy, copied from books I'd borrowed from the library, and could identify all the major organs from the heart and lungs to the kidneys, and all their complex functions. Encouraged by my father, I gained entrance to the prestigious college of Chartres, and began what was to become an illustrious career as a surgeon. My future was assured, and my reputation guaranteed to open the doors to society. Until, that is, an unfortunate incident which changed everything and took my life on a perilous course.

The familiar echo of horses' hooves rang out on the cobbles beyond the hospital walls; the occasional tinkle of a bicycle bell; a reminder that the great and the good of Paris were busy going about their business. Through the barred window, a view of the hospital grounds. Several prison trustees worked in the garden, distinctive in their baggy white pantaloons and wide brimmed hats; they dug over the soil under the watchful eyes of the guards, resigned to their enforced spell of manual labour.

As a resident psychiatrist at the prison, Cousteau had treated many of the country's most notorious criminals, diagnosing their various conditions and giving evidence at their trials. Rather than be repulsed or otherwise distracted by their crimes, he took a scholarly view and thrived on the unique insights into their character that such a privileged position accorded. To Cousteau they were more than mere 'case studies', but a means of casting light upon the human condition. Many had tried to evade his skilful interrogations, sometimes with a degree of success, as he later found out to his chagrin. But generally, they responded to his sympathetic manner with enthusiasm, entrusting whole areas of their lives to him without restraint. His reputation grew accordingly, making him something of an authority in medical circles.

Duvall's case was intriguing. After leaving his room on the Boulevard Haussmann, he'd been found by a neighbour, wandering outside, with – according to his later statement – little recollection of the past few hours. He blamed his recurrent amnesia on a horse-riding accident that had left him concussed, and with a painful back injury; which, according to Duvall, was to have dire consequences later on. Having discovered the painkilling properties of morphine through his position as a surgeon, he gained direct access to an almost unlimited supply. *'Small doses of the drug gave me much needed relief for a few hours. However, it soon transpired that I'd substituted one source of discomfort for another. Within months, I'd developed a considerable dependence, which led me to steal from the hospital pharmacy in order to maintain a certain equilibrium.'* This theft went on for several months, until Duvall's recklessness in procuring the drug brought him to the attention of the departmental head. Thus began his ignominious fall from grace and eventual dismissal.

Duvall's personal account was extremely revealing. With these words, written in Duvall's fastidious handwriting, Cousteau could add to the profile he'd already built from the police report and the prison doctor's assessment. Duvall clearly had a high opinion of himself, perhaps deservedly so given his background. The case itself had received widespread coverage in the press. Many of his claims had been refuted by the medical establishment, several of whom had been eager to denounce him as a charlatan. That he had at one time studied medicine in Paris was beyond dispute – the records of Chartres proved this to be true. But from here the details were inconsistent. The notoriety of the case and the resulting media speculation blurred the lines between fact and fiction. During this time, Duvall himself became something of a celebrity, his former profession and high standing earning him a unique fascination among the public. Women, especially, seemed to find him particularly engaging.

Duvall's imminent arrival prompted a frisson of excitement, an unusual response given Cousteau's usually stoic temperament. He rang down for Lauren, and asked for the escort detail to be sent up as soon as it arrived.

'Is there anything else, Doctor?' Lauren said.

A minor pang of conscience stirred his memory.

'How's the child?' he said.

'He's a little better now, thank you. His fever has passed and he's eating again.'

'That must be a great relief for you, Lauren. Have the escort come up right away, will you?'

The police report detailed Duvall's first foray into the criminal underworld, which ultimately was to become his undoing. Having swapped the surgeon's scalpel for a six-inch blade, he began to frequent the bars and the bordellos of the Latin Quarter, looking for drugs and the means to make a living among the dispossessed. This information added an extra element to Duvall's character that was harder to understand. The press had seized upon it, using it to further sensationalise the details of the case, and to paint Duvall in a monstrous light.

And yet, as the facts emerged, it appeared to be a simple crime of passion, a love story that had gone tragically wrong. Having developed an interest in Duvall's mistress – the notorious courtesan, Véronique, Lord Hamilton appeared to have replaced Duvall in her affections. According to witnesses, Duvall had erupted in a 'blazing fury', vowing to take his revenge.

Cousteau returned to the handwritten account, written like a memoir in Duvall's flamboyant prose.

I was born, Maurice Edmund Duvall, in a Paris tenement in 1856. My parents were ordinary citizens, wealthy but without ostentation. My earliest memory is being carried on my father's broad shoulders and tipped headfirst into the sea during a holiday in Biarritz, an experience that has always stayed with me as a reminder of the perilous and somewhat arbitrary nature of childhood. My mother was an artist and a thespian, whose preoccupations were centred largely around the theatre. Her beauty was of the wild and irrepressible type, her temperament that of a spirited colt that refused to be broken. My father was as exasperated as he was consumed by her, and spent most of his time and earnings trying to live up to her grand expectations.

During my internship at the College of Chartres, and later studying under the great Auguste Nélaton in Paris, I learned the skills that would later make me famous; I once carried out a hazardous three-hour operation on a five-year-old boy. He survived, due largely to decisions I had taken under some duress, and was returned to his grateful parents some time later. The success of the operation, and my obvious brilliance, became the subject of great speculation among both my colleagues, and leaders in the field. I, in turn, became something of a celebrity, heralded as the new savant of surgical procedures. I ate at all the best restaurants and had drinks sent to my table. This sudden fame, however, wasn't to last.

A sharp knock at the door brought Cousteau back to the present moment.

'Come in?'

Lauren entered with a look of barely-suppressed anticipation.

'The escort has arrived, Doctor.'

'Send them in, will you?'

Moments later, escorted by two burly prison guards, the infamous former surgeon, Maurice Duvall, made his entrance. He stood, rather stiffly, composed and alert, but with the faintest glimmer of humour as he took in his new surroundings.

'Thank you,' Cousteau said, dismissing the guards; they responded with some confusion.

'Our orders were to stay with the prisoner at all times,' one said.

'That won't be necessary. You may remain outside until I call you.'

Reluctantly, the guards left, closing the door behind them. Cousteau felt no fear in Duvall's presence, only the stirrings of a professional curiosity. Here was a man who once belonged to a similar class as his own, and who, perhaps due to unfortunate circumstances, had been reduced to the status of a common criminal.

His first impressions were of a rather elegant fellow. Unlike the prisoners working in the garden, Duvall's neat grey jacket and matching waistcoat gave him the look of a banker or a businessman, a man of refinement and taste. Behind the round, steel-framed spectacles, was a steely and intelligent gaze. No trace of the terrible crime he'd been accused of.

'Please, take a seat,' Cousteau said, indicating the chair on the other side of his desk. Duvall obliged, lowering himself into the seat with a grimace.

'Are you in pain?' Cousteau said.

'I have a long-standing back condition that restricts my movements. I try not to let it hinder me too much. There are worse things, I'm sure.'

With Duvall seated, they could begin. Cousteau glanced over the report on his desk, that summarised the details of the case and forthcoming trial, for which the renowned lawyer, Deschamps, had been assigned. Cousteau had been most impressed with the elaborate and meticulous way Deschamps had presented the murderer Foucault's defence, acknowledging his masterful oratory, which at times had held the courtroom spellbound. However, in this instance the great lawyer's efforts were to no avail. Foucault was convicted and received the death penalty for the unlawful killing of a prostitute. The case had provoked a huge outcry among the public, who flocked to the courtroom to hear the sentencing.

Duvall's case would prove a difficult challenge, given the publicity surrounding it, and the high profile of the accused sitting across from Cousteau now.

'How do you feel?' the doctor said.

'Perhaps a little inconvenienced, shall we say.'

'Is that how you view your current situation?'

'A turn of phrase, that is all. Although an apt enough description given the circumstances.'

The doctor sat back and clasped his fingers together. Duvall observed the room more closely, admiring the academic books on the shelves with their broad red spines, the disused fireplace filled with dusty ledgers.

He smiled, his interest captured suddenly.

'May I enquire as to how you came by your rather fierce-looking companion?' he said.

The doctor turned to the stuffed Golden Eagle perched upon a stand, its black eyes fixed upon an imaginary prey. 'Ah – yes. He's a fine specimen, don't you think?'

'Is he here to intimidate your patients into making a confession?'

'He was actually donated by one of my predecessors, and has been here ever since.' Cousteau indulged the moment of levity, encouraged by the start they'd made. But the need to delve a little deeper became more pressing. 'Tell me a little about your background,' he said. 'Your earliest recollections.'

Duvall took off his spectacles, and rubbed his eyes, as if the action might prompt his ability to recall. Slipping them back on, he cleared his throat and began. He talked at length in a relaxed and unhurried manner, confirming many of the details written in his autobiography. His mother seemed to feature a good deal, and when he spoke of her his voice took on a distinct, almost wistful quality. At no time did he mention his arrest, or the crime he was accused of.

'According to the account you wrote in prison,' Cousteau said, 'you were once treated by Dr Pierre Janet? How did this come about?'

Duvall sat up, and assumed an aristocratic bearing, as if mention of the name had reenergised him in some way. 'Ah, yes – the esteemed Dr Janet. This chance meeting was to prove highly instrumental in directing the course of my future, which by then hung precariously in the balance. Janet described my case as one of the most baffling and disturbing of his entire career.'

'May I ask how you met?'

We were introduced by a mutual friend at a prestigious dinner. You know the type – members of various fraternities gather to congratulate each other on their collective brilliance. My presence among them had by then lost something of its veneer.'

'I take it you're referring to your dismissal from the hospital?'

'That was later. Dr Janet listened to my account that night and said he'd like to help me. We could, if I deemed it appropriate, meet at some point and discuss further. This I agreed to. Of course, I had no idea at the time that details of this private agreement would one day be serialised in all the newspapers.'

Duvall went on to describe these 'sessions' with the esteemed psychiatrist; the series of walks they took through the city and the long discussions they had about the nature of being, and the challenge presented by neurosis. Recalling these early meetings, Duvall's tone changed, his gaze becoming distant as he stared out the window.

'By this time my marriage was falling apart, and I was suffering bouts of insomnia. Once, out walking alone, I stopped by the bridge and stared into the water, lost in some vague or imagined malaise. Unbeknown to me, Janet had arrived ahead of schedule, and, beholding my disposition, feared for my immediate safety.'

'Can you remember the cause of this particular unease?'

'I cannot. Only that the water seemed to concentrate my thoughts, causing me intense and distressing rumination.'

Encouraged by the relaxed atmosphere, and perhaps seizing the opportunity to impress, Duvall opened up even more about his past. The doctor's questions were unobtrusive and fashioned in such a way as to draw him out, a method Cousteau used successfully with other patients. Perhaps mindful of such a ruse, Duvall remained cautious, observing Cousteau with his narrow gaze, his recollections sometimes tailing off.

'Tell me what happened after your dismissal from the hospital?' Cousteau said.

'I stayed in Montmartre for a while, relying mainly upon the charity of friends.'

'Then you came back to Paris?'

'After a while. But things had changed considerably by then. My marriage ended, and so too did my prospects for gainful employment. There isn't much call for a disgraced surgeon.'

'You found other means of sustaining yourself?'

Duvall smiled at this rather obvious attempt to trick him. 'By then I'd spent years living on my wits, and had developed that instinctive sense for danger, whichever form it may take. I also had my country estate, which I'd managed to hang on to.'

Cousteau nodded vaguely, weighing the details against those in the report. Duvall's file lay open on the desk, his entire life up until that point open to dissection. Of his wanderings in the Latin

Quarter, and various other places, he'd been deliberately vague, alluding only briefly to the criminal element he'd found there. Regarding the death of Lord Hamilton he'd said nothing.

'I'd like to go back, if I may,' Cousteau said. 'Tell me about the fire that occurred in Rouen when you were a child?'

'I believe it was a paraffin-burner. My parents were asleep and never woke up.'

'Your three siblings also?'

'Yes, a terrible tragedy. I went to live with an aunt in Bordeaux.'

'Did you attend the funeral?'

'It was thought that the trauma would be too much for me. I've since pondered the wisdom of such a decision, but have had to accept it. I'm sure these things are done with the best intentions, but they leave one a little confused all the same.'

Again, the doctor nodded with apparent understanding. This episode had been glossed over in the original assessment, as if it was of little consequence. A tragedy indeed, as Duvall himself had put it, and one that had claimed the lives of his entire family. But once again, the details were clouded in mystery and open to interpretation. The implication that Duvall himself had been responsible had never really gone away.

'This *event* must have been extremely difficult for you,' Cousteau said. 'You were a child – ten or eleven years-old, I believe?'

'Perhaps that is largely a gift of providence, that it blots out such things to spare us the details. Because of this, I have very little recollection of that time whatsoever.'

Cousteau made an entry into his notebook, glancing up now and then like an artist capturing a particular shade of his subject's face. A light breeze lifted the air, the patch of blue sky a reminder of the world beyond the barred window. Duvall seemed at that time a sympathetic character, perhaps more a victim of cruel circumstance than the heinous criminal he'd been made out to be.

'Of course,' the doctor said, 'it is quite possible that your mind blocked out the details to spare you the, understandably, distressing memories. I'm familiar with many such cases involving amnesia of this sort.'

Duvall assumed a manner of courteous interest, weighing the doctor's words with a curious frown.

'However,' the doctor continued. 'there have also been criminal cases, the defence of which has relied upon a similar assertion. The accused simply claiming he was not there at the time of the incident and could not therefore be held accountable in the legal sense.'

'Are you accusing me of such a fabrication?'

Cousteau smiled and rolled his pen between his fingertips. The file on his desk seemed to beckon him, inviting further examination. 'You made a personal request to see me. Can I ask why?'

'I was sent to the hospital wing at La Santé for evaluation. The doctor there recommended that I be held for a further assessment, and, having heard of your pre-eminence in the field of psychiatry, I requested an interview with you right away.'

Cousteau nodded, aware of the obvious flattery, but enjoying it nonetheless. It seemed the strangest thing, that they were here in his book-lined study, with its view of the quaint little garden being tended by prison trustees. Such a setting must've been a welcome distraction for Duvall, having spent months on remand, cooped up in austere and often brutal conditions. And yet so far, they hadn't touched upon the real nature of the meeting – the crime of passion which had brought him to this point.

'Tell me about Véronique?'

A cloud fell across Duvall's vision. In an instant, his mood changed from agreeable to morose. He sniffed abruptly, and adjusted his waistcoat with a sharp tug.

'I have nothing to say regarding that matter.'

'May I ask why?'

'She was a part of my life I choose to forget.'

'And yet you lived for a significant period as man and wife – before ...'

The silence encompassed both the grave subject matter and the intrigue surrounding it. The newspapers had called the murder a work of 'diabolical frenzy', a headline they were to duplicate several times throughout the course of the investigation. And photographs of Duvall had appeared, earning him the epithet, 'the little surgeon.' Images of Véronique had also appeared in the papers, her glamour and beauty overshadowed by the details of her young lover's tragic demise.

'It would seem that there is a good deal of evidence against you,' Cousteau said. 'You had, by all accounts, a significant ... motive.'

Duvall sighed audibly and took a moment to reflect. 'There was a time when I'd been happy and optimistic about the future. This woman became my muse, the canvas upon which I painted, if you will. But you see, Doctor, there is a price to pay for entertaining such a fatal conceit.'

'There was some discord between you?'

'She was not, as I later discovered, who she claimed to be. There was no family chateau in Provence. No great fortune to inherit once her father died. She was to all intents, a courtesan, who used all the deviousness and cunning of her trade in order to gain advancement into higher circles.'

'Circles that included Lord Hamilton?'

Duvall smiled vaguely. And yet, something compelled him to continue. 'My memories of Véronique are tinged with sorrow. I often picture her out riding in her carriage along the Bois, wearing one of her exotic crinoline dresses, a fur over her shoulders. She had the look of nobility, you see, acquired after her long association with society's elite.' Duvall paused to consider another aspect. 'I allowed myself to be distracted from my work. That was my biggest mistake. My marriage also fell apart, my wife unable to put up with the public humiliation. To put it succinctly, I squandered a fortune on an illusion, something that simply wasn't there.'

'Were you in love with her?' Cousteau said deliberately.

Duvall pondered the question, left provocatively between them.

'I was bewitched,' he said. 'Mesmerised. I saw before me a glittering jewel of inestimable value, which I simply had to have.'

'A price for which you paid heavily?'

Duvall looked away, unable or unwilling to answer.

Cousteau pictured the scene, this once proud and successful

man reduced to the status of a bankrupt because of his obsession for a woman. He'd come across men like this before, often of previous good standing, who'd lost the ability to reason. Their souls, as it were, gone to the devil.

Perhaps this was a feature of the case previously ignored. A temporary insanity, which, while serving as no defence in a court of law, would certainly explain the subject's uncharacteristic behaviour. Similar crimes of passion had been committed since time began. Men of previous high standing, like Duvall, had gone to the guillotine because of just such an aberration.

Turning to Duvall's file, he scanned a section of the handwritten account, absorbing Duvall's own words: *I was not amused. Inwardly, I cursed the system under which I'd fallen foul. All because I'd taken up with a treacherous woman, who betrayed me and brought the gendarmes to my door. Now my life is over, consigned to a grim dungeon, where the only glimpse of the world is through a barred window.* Cousteau stopped reading. Duvall had been a model prisoner, by all accounts. Such was the regard held for him by the prison authorities, that he'd been given privileges and been made a trustee. Instead of a prison cell with hardened convicts, he had his own room in the prison hospital. He was even permitted to wear his own clothes.

And yet the police report claimed a different, more vengeful side to him. Turning to this, Cousteau identified a particularly incriminating passage.

'The inspector leading the case said that when confronted, you showed no remorse.'

'How does one feel remorse for something one cannot recall?'

'Did you not confess to the murder at one point? And did you not during the course of your interrogation claim that you also intended to kill Véronique?'

'On the contrary. The police fabricated a statement in order to convince the chief prosecutor that he had a case. I have always maintained my innocence, and will continue to do so until I'm completely exonerated.' Duvall's indignation lit-up his entire being. He became charged, as it were, with a discernible passion that altered his physique. Cousteau was reminded of the famous actor, Maloir, who'd been charged with embezzlement, and how his courtroom appearances were like inspired performances on the stage, attracting queues of admirers to the public gallery.

'How do you feel about her now? I know she made some rather unflattering comments about you to the press.'

Duvall shrugged. 'I'm a surgeon. To sustain such a level of concentration under conditions of immense pressure, one needs an almost ruthless disregard for the opinions of others.'

'You bear her no ill will?'

'She means nothing to me. Nothing at all.'

Cousteau steered the conversation to less contentious areas. What had Duvall's life been like during the height of his success? The strolls by the Seine, sipping cognac in the bars and cafes with his wealthy and celebrated friends. Probing delicately, Cousteau began again, aware that they were adversaries on opposite sides of an invisible line. By observing the formalities like gentlemen, each was looking to exploit the other's weakness and by doing so, gain an advantage.

'During the hearing, your background was questioned quite rigorously,' Cousteau said, pausing to let the inference sink in. 'It was suggested that you somehow "invented" your tenure at Chartres, and were in fact expelled due to certain thefts from the pharmacy. I have the original transcript here ...' As if to underscore his point, he held up the document that lay on his desk.

'Many such claims were made against me,' Duvall said with contempt, 'with the sole intention of destroying my character. But my professional qualifications speak for themselves. As a surgeon I had no equal.'

Cousteau lay the incriminating document down, and assumed an air of quiet deliberation. The pleasant ring of pick and shovel drifted up from the work detail below; the men worked methodically, absorbed in their labours.

'The trial date is a few weeks away,' Cousteau said. 'I'm sure you're aware that should you be convicted by a jury, you face the guillotine. Does such a prospect concern you?'

'Not in the least. I would consider it an honour to face such an outcome in a composed and dignified manner.'

The doctor reflected on these words, and the persuasive nature of Duvall's response. The prison doctor's report stated *homicidal monomania.* Perhaps there was indeed some hidden mental disorder which could account for Duvall's apparent detachment and lack of concern.

'What of your wife, your family?' he said.

'They have disowned me already. I have been abandoned, left to my fate.'

Cousteau adjusted his posture, drawing himself up in his chair. An irresistible sense of destiny seized him. He pictured himself in the courtroom, giving evidence on Duvall's behalf. How the press would trumpet his name in all the papers. His colleagues would all give a collective bow in respect of his knowledge and ability.

'Were you to consider helping me,' he said, 'your cooperation would be taken into account and would, undoubtedly, weigh in your favour. But you would have to be, shall we say, more revealing.'

Duvall's eyes glinted with the promise of fresh opportunity. 'If I was to consider such an offer,' he said, 'would it mean the granting of further privileges? Extended visits, perhaps? Access to certain law books that would assist in preparation for my trial?'

'I would certainly make such an application on your behalf.'

Duvall pondered, smoothing his chin between thumb and forefinger. 'Perhaps my immediate future is not as cut and dried as I'd anticipated – if you will pardon my little pun. And yet so much rests on your report, does it not?'

'I will submit my report to the judge in due course. In the meantime, is there anything else you need.'

'Yes, there is one thing. Perhaps I may be permitted a pen and some writing paper? I have some letters I wish to compose. The last requests I made were refused without an explanation. I was most disappointed.'

'The granting of requests is not within my jurisdiction, I'm afraid. I can but make an application on your behalf.'

The doctor understood Duvall's reasoning. As a celebrated

surgeon he was known throughout the land for saving the lives of countless wealthy patients, many of whom wrote to thank him personally. So it was entirely natural for him to consider himself above all the petty rules and regulations that bound the rest of the prison population.

'There is one other thing,' Duvall said.

'Go on.'

'If the circumstances were favourable, I should like to be included in the work detail. Is this something you could recommend?'

The doctor paused, observing Duvall closely. His request seemed a little unusual, given his current predicament.

'Is there anything in particular that interests you?'

'I should like to tend the hospital garden, if I may. I find the open air most invigorating. And a certain amount of movement is good for my physical condition.'

'I will need to speak to the commissioner,' Cousteau said. Then, feeling the need to further placate Duvall in some way, added, 'I will make a full report stating how cooperative you have been, recommending that you be granted the privileges you have requested.'

'Thank you, Doctor. I appreciate your assistance.'

Cousteau looked at the clock. An hour had passed relatively quickly.

'I should like to see you again,' he said. 'Provided you are in agreement, of course?'

'It would be my absolute pleasure. I remain, as it were, your captive audience.'

Cousteau called for the guards, and Duvall was taken away.

And so began a series of regular interviews between Duvall and the doctor, whose observations were recorded in his journal. He began to look forward to the sessions, and the stimulating conversations they had, coming to see Duvall more as an equal than a patient. And on his recommendation, Duvall's privileges were increased, including his request to be assigned to the gardening detail. He was, Cousteau attested in his report to the commissioner, a model prisoner, who presented no threat to prison security.

With less than a week to go before the trial, a sense of urgency fell upon them. Here they were, the esteemed doctor and the alleged murderer, engaging in a civilised discussion in his comfortable little office, medical volumes lining the shelves, and the rapacious Golden Eagle perched rather disconcertingly in the corner. Only the unseen presence of the two guards outside the door alluded to the seriousness of the situation and Duvall's high profile status. Cousteau, who'd made his reputation through the detached and rigorous examination of madness in all its varied forms; who'd stood up in courtrooms and delivered his findings to the jury, who hung on to his every word. And Duvall, the model prisoner, whose crime had shocked the nation, making him, as he'd previously stated, the most notorious figure in the whole of France.

And yet, over time, Duvall's outwardly genial manner began to disturb the doctor somewhat. There was no suggestion of any congenital impairment, which might have caused a later degeneration in his thinking and behaviour. No apparent history of hereditary illness which may also have had a bearing. Reading over the various reports, and meeting Duvall in person had convinced him that the patient was indeed sound of mind and body, and therefore perfectly able to stand trial for the crime he was accused of committing: the murder of the flamboyant young lord, who had very publicly humiliated Duvall and stolen his mistress.

But by now they had reached a mutual understanding. Because of his good conduct, and the report Cousteau had submitted to his superiors, the close security that had been placed around Duvall had been relaxed. No longer chained like other inmates, he was permitted small privileges unavailable to the majority of the prison population. He could continue to wear his own clothes, sparing him the indignity of the demeaning striped cottons worn by convicted prisoners. Such was the impact of his appearance on those who chanced upon him for the first time, that many were astonished to learn of his true identity. The prison governor himself once mistook Duvall for a lawyer and enquired as to whom he was visiting.

However, there was still the issue of Duvall's feelings towards Véronique, a subject that bothered Cousteau a great deal. Their discussions concerning her had rarely been illuminating, except in Duvall's sometimes monosyllabic response when confronted. There in the doctor's office, Duvall could not hide, compelled to answer questions he would rather avoid, if only to further his claim of innocence in the death of the young lord.

And yet, Cousteau continued, pressing Duvall gently but firmly, determined to uncover the truth. His persistence paid off. At times, Duvall's composure would slip. He would allude to deeper, more complex feelings of animosity towards her, rather than towards the young man whose life he was accused of taking. Cousteau was left with the unavoidable, and troubling, conclusion, that within Duvall there lurked a murderous rage.

And so it came to their final session, scheduled for later that afternoon. Cousteau felt a strange disappointment that their brief acquaintanceship would soon be over. The next time they met would be in a packed courtroom, where both prosecution and defence would begin their cases.

The light outside was already starting to dim, the prison blocks' rooftops outlined against the grey sky; a glimpse of the neat little garden beneath the window, which offered Cousteau a peculiar but affecting solace. The work party were packing away their tools, preparing to leave. Cousteau looked for Duvall, by now accustomed to seeing his slight, almost unassuming figure working alongside the other trustees. And yet, as they were escorted away by the guards, it appeared that Duvall was not among them.

Trying to ignore his initial alarm, Cousteau called down to Lauren.

'Could you check that monsieur Duvall was scheduled for this afternoon's work party?'

'Yes, of course.'

'And that he has a four o'clock appointment with me?'

'I can confirm that now. I wrote it in the ledger.'

A shrill whistle blast rang out from the courtyard. Hurrying to the window, Cousteau looked out. A commotion of some sort had broken out. Several prison warders ran towards the heavy gates that led to the admin buildings. More strident whistle blasts followed, ringing out across the courtyard with a sense of urgency.

Unable to draw himself away, Cousteau watched, an awful feeling of premonition rising within him.

A sharp rap at the door startled him.

Lauren burst in uninvited. She stood there, breathless, her face red with exertion.

'Monsieur Duvall ... He's killed a guard and absconded!'

Cousteau opened his mouth to speak but no words came. He beheld Lauren with a terrible fascination. How could such a thing happen? Duvall was supposed to be out with the work party. Cousteau had signed the papers himself.

Shouts echoed across the courtyard. Urgent cries for assistance, sharp commands directed to subordinates.

Cousteau sank into his chair, dimly aware of Lauren's presence. It seemed at that moment as if his entire world had been torn from its axis.

'What shall I do?' Lauren said. 'The commissioner will demand an explanation.'

Cousteau remained in his chair, vaguely aware of the activity outside the window. Already, Duvall's escape had caused a huge disruption to the monotony of prison life. Word would be broadcast to the remotest corners. Soon everyone would know.

For Cousteau there could only be one outcome. All those hours he'd spent poring over Duvall's motives, analysing his character, his background. The murderous rage he'd identified, and yet neglected to include in his reports because of his own vaunted self-interest.

His career was finished. Worse still, the ridicule he would face from colleagues, who would see through the whole charade and blame him entirely. He would never have his day in court. Never again get to impress the jury with his meticulous evaluations.

His gaze was drawn to the corner of the room. There, on its perch, was the Golden Eagle, talons extended, black eyes fixed upon its unsuspecting prey. Duvall's eyes. The eyes of a killer.

And now Cousteau would have the blood of an innocent on his hands. For Duvall had surely escaped to fulfil his original diabolical intention. To take revenge on his former mistress, Véronique.

California Gold

The story went that he was a thief and she was a liar, that they somehow got together because of certain quirks in their character that made such unions possible. But that wasn't the whole truth, or even a respectable part of it. They were simply two people who'd connected at a basic level, and realised that the sum of two forces combined was stronger than one on its own. And used in the promotion of certain business ventures – for reasons of pure self-interest, of course – such a combination could yield a rich and satisfying harvest. But they could never look back, or like Lot's wife they'd be turned to a pillar of salt. Why look back anyway, when your life was a fireworks display of spectacular proportions? There were new people to meet, parties to go to, and the whole world looking on in wonder.

The girl, Peaches, celebrated 21 years on the planet, an achievement she viewed with some reluctance. As the million-dollar face of Chanel, hers was a homespun appeal, an easy style and natural beauty uncommon to those not born with it. The countless agents and hangers-on who frequented her world, saw her as a commodity, a mysterious and exotic wild bird of limitless value, that resisted all attempts at being enslaved. Having reached the heights of her profession at such a tender age, she was already 'battle hardened', a consummate professional who knew exactly what the industry expected of her and how to respond.

With cameras flashing, and all eyes in the house trained in her direction, she strode the catwalks of Milan, Paris and New York, a living sculpture cloaked in the latest McQueen or Versace. With her platinum blonde hair and long, slender limbs, she stood out, even amongst the gazelles that grazed on the great plains, smiling coyly for the press. Some said it was her eyes, a magnetic blue-grey that radiated a dazzling cinematic light. Others that it was the voice of honeyed velvet that whispered casually in the ear of a starstruck admirer, who'd turn to find she'd gone, vanished into the night.

The boy, Dino, had an essentially male charm, complete with chiselled jawline and languid hand gesture. With his greased-back hair and Latin good looks, he, too, stood out in the crowd. His easy-going manner and inner confidence, gave him a detached and alluring air. Like Peaches, his dreams were visionary and impulsive – plus, he had a job most men would kill for, shooting the world's most beautiful women, and putting them on the covers of the world's most prestigious magazines. Out here in California, with the palm trees and the haciendas, all that glittered was indeed gold. But he never once forgot where he came from. What it was like for a family of six to live crowded in one room, and to have your ass whipped regularly by the street gangs on your way home from school.

Cruising California's Pacific Coast Highway in the rented open top, the warm breeze whipped Peaches' hair across her face. They played their favourite game, a variation of the fantasy scenario that ran on all kinds of weird tangents.

'What would you do if I went to Nova Scotia without telling you?' Peaches said.

'Why Nova Scotia?'

'I don't know. It just sorta popped into my head.'

Dino gazed out at the Pacific coast, and thought about buying a yacht.

'I'd come looking for you and kill the guy you were with,' he said.

'Who said I was with anyone?'

'I was taking it as a given.'

'You'd really kill someone for me?'

'I'd do it as a matter of honour, because I couldn't stand to see you with someone else.'

Dino allowed his thoughts to wander to some remote plateau; beside him, the Coppertone strip of Peaches' thigh to act as a distraction. Far below, angry waves crashed against the rocks, throwing up cascades of phosphorous spray. The games he and Peaches played had a strange significance, bonding them together in ways he couldn't fathom. The guy they met, who went with them to their motel, having produced a bag of high-grade cocaine as an introduction. These transient assignations didn't mean anything – at least not to Peaches. She had a practical, almost competitive attitude to sex, just as she did most other things. It served a purpose, relieving her physical needs and the tension that built up from her job, something that could be discarded later, like an empty soda bottle tossed out onto the highway after use.

Sometimes Dino struggled to keep up with her. Sometimes it seemed he'd become a bystander, watching her star soar ever higher. She thrived on a diet of the superficial, a moment-by-moment adjustment to wherever they happened to be, and whatever lurid distractions were available. Discussions of art and literature passed her by, of no use and little value. If there was something missing it could always be supplied up ahead, at the next location, the next big party. But he needed her like an addict needs a drug, and like all addicts, he simply stopped fighting and gave in to his addiction.

'How do you feel on your big day?' he said.

'Great ... Why?'

'I thought you might feel different. You know, now that you're that much older.'

'Not as old as you. That *would* be something, wouldn't it!'

Twenty-one years on the planet, a milestone that filled Peaches with a mixture of awe and trepidation. Born in Sheffield, England, she saw herself as Californian at heart; the weather, the people and the beaches suited her temperament – three hundred days sunshine a year and great golf courses! Plenty of opportunity to practice her handicap and beat her dad, who thought he was the best at everything. But it was her dad who'd instilled in her the spirit of competition, so she had him to thank for that. England appealed to her as a vague reminder of Christmas, and family outings to Blackpool and Morecombe when she was a child. She had grand ideas and vision, thinking always of herself first, as she'd been trained to do from an early age. Dino had a similar outlook, an aspect that'd attracted her to him in the first place. As a couple, they drew people into their orbit, whether at poolside parties or simply walking the street. They had what it takes – whatever *that* was – and they knew how to use it.

The previous few years had passed by in a haze of hotel rooms and jetlag, modelling for the likes of L'Oréal and Chanel. She'd been introduced to another life – the partying and the networking, emerging from a club in the grey dawn and adjusting to the light like a vampire. The lifestyle consumed her; the catwalks and the other girls, all of them on a vibrant carousel that whirled them round 24/7. She couldn't stop now even if she wanted to. Sometimes it felt like a whole industry had sprung up around her. All she had to do was turn up and do her thing.

'So what's the surprise?' she said. 'Where are you taking me?'

'Nowhere. This is it.'

She frowned, and rearranged her hat in the drop down mirror.

'I need a holiday,' she said.

'We're in California!'

'Everyone needs a break. I've been working myself too hard lately, in case you hadn't noticed.'

'How about we book in to the Chateau Marmont and check out the ghost of John Belushi?'

'I'm trying to be serious. I'm 21 now. Doesn't that mean anything to you?'

'OK – how about we drive over to see Hyman instead?'

The name conjured its own brand of intrigue, especially to Peaches, who always remembered their first introduction at the Hemingway Bar in Paris.

'We haven't seen him for months,' she said. 'How do you even know he'll be in?'

'I'll call him. Once he knows it's your birthday he'll drop everything – just for you, honey.'

The idea began to appeal more and more. Hyman was the original mover and shaker, someone who'd helped her when she'd first arrived in LA. He knew everyone, and was always first on the guest list of people who wanted to be seen.

Dino started to tell a story about New York bath houses in the 80s. She listened with a morbid fascination, thinking of the designers she knew, who were all gay.

'They used to have these orgies back in the 80s,' he said, 'before AIDS kicked-in. You could literally wander in off the street and have sex with hundreds of men.'

'What's that got to do with Hyman?'

'He's a fruit ... Maricon. Likes to take it in the ass.'

And so their humorous exchanges continued, as they headed further out on Highway 1. The same winding blacktop that famous movie stars once cruised in their open top convertibles, faces tanned and flawlessly made-up for the big screen. Peaches felt a dreamy nostalgia for this bygone era, but was far too caught up in the drama of her own life to bother too much with something that was gone forever and could never be recaptured. But she loved *Rebecca*, and watched it over and over, becoming obsessed with the actress Joan Fontaine.

Dino pulled over to call Hyman. Peaches watched from the passenger seat, wishing she could drive. American cars had a character all of their own, but they drank juice like nothing else. Someday the money would run out and they'd be forced to do one of two things – either go back to England, or stay in California and hustle. Hustling was the modern-day equivalent of panhandling for Gold in the Black Hills, something that had a vague, romantic association in her head; some people were naturally suited to it and made fortunes. Others toiled for hours in the hot sun, never breaking even, always dreaming of the time they'd defy the odds and make it big.

But poverty remained one of Peaches' biggest fears. The wealth she'd accumulated in such a short time would run out and she'd be forced to work for a living. No more exotic shoots for American *Vogue* or *Tatler*. No more designer pieces from Prada and Yamamoto. The frightening thing about money was its alarming tendency to disappear. The huge sums she earned as a model were obscured by the inevitable complications that arose as a result. The team of experts and financial advisers she employed helped her keep track of it all, securing viable investments in stocks and property that would hold their own and not depreciate in time. The whole thing bored the living shit out of her, but she knew she had to keep on top of it. And the arguments she had with her dad. He knew better than they did, of course, and tried to interfere all the time. Anyone would think he was a fucking accountant!

Dino climbed into the driver side, and sat there without saying anything.

'Did you speak to him?' she said.

'Sorry honey. I told him today's your birthday, but he just said, so what?' Dino gave her his blank look. 'Maybe he thinks you're not that special.'

She read the look on his face, and shrieked with pleasure.

'Liar!'

Dino grinned, and kissed her on the cheek. 'He's down by the pool now, waiting for us to join him!'

Peaches felt a little thrill of anticipation. Hyman's Roman villa, with its marble porticos and sumptuous garden – plus the most beautiful bathroom she'd ever seen! Hyman had introduced her to John Galiano at the Café Tabac, the night she got drunk and tripped over a chair in front of hundreds of people. Hyman, whose parties were known all over town. People gravitated to him naturally, seduced by his aura. Women loved him, and wanted to be near him, endlessly amused by his outrageous comments and acid putdowns.

Dino took the next bend in the road like a racing driver, his face frozen in concentration. The crystalline blue of the Santa Barbara coast stretched far below them in a widescreen panoramic shot. Peaches loved this part of California, its restful, dreamlike quality, the awesome power of the waves that crashed against the rocks in perfect slow-motion.

She glanced across at Dino, thinking how ridiculously good-looking he was without even trying.

'Do you think Hyman will introduce me to Harry ?' she said.

'What do you want to be introduced to him for?'

'I don't know. He might be useful.'

'for what?'

'I'm just thinking out loud. Fuck. Stop analysing everything I say!'

Dino enjoyed her reaction. The fine lines of that famous profile, traced from the gently sloping brow to the tip of her nose and sensual curve of her mouth. The epitome of all things desirable, but the promise cleverly withheld. That combination of allure and elusiveness that men found irresistible; the long, tanned legs and flimsy tops, modest breasts and pert nipples; she rarely wore a bra, preferring the freedom it gave her.

On they went, past the mansions on the clifftop, wealthy enclaves hidden behind the electronic gates and the bougainvillea, where even the paparazzi couldn't get a look in. And there, in one such dwelling, lounging by the pool like a modern day Al Capone in his silky red bathrobe and carpet slippers, was the corpulent figure of Hyman himself.

Sun glinting on his gold rings, he welcomed his guests with arms wide. To Hyman they were the children he'd never had. He could indulge them in so many ways – especially Peaches, whose career he'd followed closely, claiming, with some legitimacy, to have discovered her in a night club in Milan. For Hyman knew the secret of success, that in the end it was the province of a select few, a river that flowed ever onward, regardless of the fluctuations of the economy or the fortunes of lesser beings who made up the majority. There were strict rules in place; the watchful eyes of the gods who decided those that prospered and those that fell by the wayside. You could never become complacent, or it might be you joining the homeless on Sunset Strip.

With the hugs and kisses over, Hyman stepped back to admire them both.

'How's the best-looking couple in LA?' he said, biting on a cigar to further his Capone image. 'Have you called to pay me back the 500 dollars you borrowed the last time you were here?'

Peaches sidled up to him, and slipped a hand beneath his arm, linking them both in a parody of affection. 'We thought we'd come over and tie you up in the basement, Hyman. Steal some of the money you keep in that safe of yours.'

'Sorry to disappoint you, sweetie. I don't keep money in the safe anymore, it's all in offshore investments. Now – how about we start with the drinks first, then you can tell me all about your latest adventure?'

Peaches let go of his arm and gave him a peevish look.

'Haven't you forgotten something?' she said.

Hyman frowned, and rubbed his chin. 'I should've put some clothes on – is that what you mean?'

Dino grinned, enjoying Hyman's expert baiting. Peaches picked up on the vibe, and decided to play along with it. She crossed her arms and tapped her foot, staring out at the distant ocean.

'OK, I get it,' she said. 'You're just going to ignore me. I'll go lie by the pool instead.'

Hyman spread his arms in a sudden gesture of benevolence. 'Hey! Hey! What do you take me for? You think I'd forget a day like this?' He flashed Dino a staged look of appeal. 'Dino, help me out here, will you? Is it something we're supposed to be celebrating here, or what?'

'I'm not sure, Hyman. Maybe it's someone's anniversary or something.'

And with that, the party began in earnest, minus the champagne and the limousines which would all come later – an organised birthday bash that Peaches wasn't supposed to know about. Hyman's housekeeper, Rosa, brought out a tray of drinks, and set it down on the ornate table by the pool. Withdrawing silently, she headed back to the house, a tireless, dark-eyed workhorse devoted exclusively to her employer.

They sat beneath the parasol, sunlight glancing from the surface of the pool. In the background, perched atop the rise, was Hyman's villa, bought with the proceeds from the many rock bands he'd discovered and helped to promote all over the civilised world. With its porticos and tiered levels, it looked out over the Pacific Ocean. At night, all lit-up from the inside, it glowed like the embers of a fire. When describing it to visitors, Hyman referred to it as 'Romanesque', because it sounded impressive. The house, or the villa, had class, and everyone who set eyes on it agreed.

Hyman stretched out his legs, that were white like the rest of his body, but carpeted with a layer of fine black hairs. 'So ...' he said, ejecting a funnel of cigar smoke from the side of his mouth. 'How does it feel to be saying goodbye to your youth, as you head towards middle age?'

Peaches frowned in objection.

'Careful, Hyman,' Dino said, 'it's a sensitive issue.'

'What's the problem? Coupla strokes from the master and all the lines disappear. That right, Peaches?'

'I don't have any lines,' she said, ignoring Hyman's reference to Kevyn, the Rembrandt of cosmetics who made goddesses of them all. She thought instead of the surprise party Dino had planned for her later; she'd picked up snippets from her girlfriends, but had pretended not to hear. A kind of hush-hush atmosphere existed that only advertised their devious intentions all the more.

'Anyway,' she said airily. 'It's just another day.'

'Wait till you get to my age,' Hyman said. 'Some days I need help to get outta the fucking chair. Then bits of you start packing up and you have to get new ones ... You know who the wealthiest people are in LA? Plastic surgeons. They write their own cheques.'

'Actually, Hyman, I wanted to ask your advice.'

'You think I got where I am today by giving free advice?' Hyman threw up his hands in mock exasperation. 'Jesus Christ. What you kids need is the firm hand of guidance – which is another thing altogether. Now *that* I can do, but it comes with interest like everything else.'

It amused Hyman to refer to the glamorous couple as 'kids', and to treat them with the forbearance of an affectionate parent. Peaches in turn treated him like a generous uncle, a kindly benefactor who would always go out of his way to do things for her, things that could never be repaid in any way.

'Come on, then,' he said. 'As it's your birthday I'll give you a free shot. Ask me anything you like.'

'I thought you said Harry could get me into the movies?'

'Harry's a busy man. What happened to that audition he got you for *The Next Big Thing*?'

'She didn't get it,' Dino said. 'They thought she was too English, whatever that means.'

Hyman nodded solemnly. 'Maybe you should do some porn instead. A nice tasteful girl on girl number to get your started. We could even shoot it here at my place. What do you think, Dino?'

'I don't have a problem with that at all, Hyman.'

'You're both being boring,' Peaches said, 'Maybe I should call up a few of my friends and go out with them instead.'

Peaches feigned a regal indifference to their good-natured mockery, used to being the centre of everyone's attention wherever she happened to be. She revelled in the attention. Even among the girls on the runway, preening and strutting like a high-end accessory, she wanted to be the best. The hotels, the partying and the jetlag, all combined to make a nonstop relay of events. Life was a giant billboard, upon which someone had affixed her face, without her doing anything other than pouting for the camera. Dino said she combined the angelic with a hint of pure decadence, a Greek goddess with a modern makeover. She liked the fact that her boyfriend was one of the top fashion photographers in the world and could have any woman he wanted. The way he looked at her sometimes made her stomach flip, like she might go crazy.

Of course, she could never even consider the alternative industry that'd sprung up in California in the 80s. The stars themselves had acquired a certain notorious mystique, rising to the top of their profession with a mixture of guile, overt sexuality and unabashed ambition. By performing brazenly in front of the camera, they did what most people would only consider doing behind closed doors. Being a keen exhibitionist, used to showing off the contours of her famous body, Peaches had no problem with the concept itself. But there were other consequences to consider. What if her dad found out, and came looking for her with a shotgun? And all that explaining she'd have to do to her family. In the end, all her sexual peccadillos were confined to her private members club, where no one could 'out' her to the press.

The swinging scene was different. She'd indulged a few times with Dino, usually at his instigation – and often after the added enticement of booze and cocaine. Dino's particular thing was to find another girl willing to join them in a threeway, something Peaches threw herself into with abandon. Occasionally, they branched out and included another couple, who had to pass Peaches' exacting rules of engagement. Dino loved seeing her in a wild state of frenzy, her long limbs splayed out on the hotel bed, or wherever it was they happened to be. Sometimes he got funny about it later, and they argued. She told him straight, she couldn't deal with him *and* his jealousy, but he couldn't seem to help it, so they stopped doing it for a while.

Now, luxuriating by the pool, with Hyman's 'Romanesque' villa in the background, she could relax and enjoy her Big Day. Later, there'd be a huge party, something she wasn't supposed to know about. The thought made her tingle with anticipation.

'By the way,' Hyman said casually. 'I've got something for you up at the house.'

'For me?' Peaches looked suitably bemused.

'For you, honey. Go take a look.'

'What is it?'

'It's just a little something, that's all.'

They watched Peaches stroll up the steps to the house, past the colourful expanse of bougainvillea to the marble columns that guarded the entrance.

'You got her a present,' Dino said. 'That's a nice touch.'

Hyman turned to him with an expression of concern. 'Is she OK? I've been telling her to take it easy for years now.'

'You know how she is, Hyman. She never stops. Always on the move, always doing something.'

'And how about you? I mean, you're both living the life, travelling all over the world, right? It takes its toll.'

'I'm pretty good. I feel lucky most days. I got everything I need.'

Dino struggled to make conversation when Peaches wasn't there. He found Hyman a little intimidating, although in fairness that was more down to his own reservations and nothing Hyman said or did. But he couldn't help feeling excluded when the two of them were together, like an observer allowed a ringside seat at a carnival. Peaches loved Hyman because he treated her like a princess and did things like buy her little treats, and introduce her to the many influential people he knew; one night they went out with one of the LA rock bands he'd signed, and all got pleasantly wasted on the Strip. Dino understood that the problem lay with himself and his volatile nature. At 32 he was that much older than Peaches. If he wasn't careful he'd alienate her and cause her to move on, a thought that ate away at him, consuming more and more of his thinking.

'At least the two of you look like you're getting on,' Hyman said. 'The last time I saw you she wanted to tear your fucking head off.'

Dino laughed. 'What's new? We argue all the time.'

'She's feisty, huh?'

'That's one way of describing her.'

'An enigma.'

'Yeah, she's that, too.'

Movement up at the house. They looked up to see a vision in red appear, her long, tanned legs negotiating the steps on the way down. Hyman's gift to Peaches, who wore the bodycon dress he'd bought her like it'd been made exclusively for her.

'Wow!' Hyman said. 'Ain't that a picture? ... Before she comes back, is everything set for tonight? Her friends all got the invites I sent out?'

'It's all taken care of. Did you organise the cake?'

'Oh – wait till you see it. It's just about the most outrageous thing you've ever seen!'

Peaches made her way across the garden towards them. Dino blinked, and raised his sunglasses to get a better look. The red dress accentuated the curves of Peaches' body, the lissom waste and pert breasts, the thoroughbred thighs that flexed a hint of muscle with every step. Sometimes her beauty mesmerised him. He'd spent years shooting the best looking women in the world, and yet each time he saw Peaches was like the first, a lightning bolt that struck him from head to foot.

Peaches joined them by the pool, and did a little twirl for Hyman, hand on hip.

'What do you think?' she said.

Hyman clapped his hands in admiration. 'My work is done! You look absolutely sensational.'

Peaches leaned over and kissed him on the cheek, stepping back with an expansive grin. She turned to Dino, almost as an afterthought.

'What's the matter – don't you like it?'

'It looks great.'

'Don't fall over yourself with enthusiasm, will you?'

But even Dino's somewhat muted response couldn't diminish Peaches enthusiasm. She sauntered alongside the pool, doing her best walk, rocking her hips to an imaginary audience. At 5' 9", she had a willowy and sinuous grace, having perfected her 'strut' on the runways of Milan, Paris and New York. Her first agent said she was too headstrong and undisciplined to make a career out of modelling, but she defied predictions and was signed fortuitously to the legendary Models 1.

'How's your handicap coming along?' Hyman said, thinking of an interview he'd read in a golfing magazine.

'Improving all the time,' she said. 'In fact I was thinking of having my birthday party at Pebble Beach so I could get some practice in.'

Peaches love of the sport came, perhaps, from her father, who had an impressive handicap of 16, and claimed he was never more than a few feet from the green at any one time. As to Peaches' natural ability, people liked to draw comparisons; Harry called her the next Jeannie Carmen, whom he used to know back in the halcyon days of the Kennedys and Frank Sinatra. Jeannie modelled clothing and hit trick shots that blew people's minds. She could hit a flagpole at 350 yards, looking like a million dollars at the same time. Peaches had a similar natural talent, and a hunger for the game that defied explanation.

Hyman's cell phone rang on the table; his pride and joy, a Nokia 3110, manufactured in Hungary, with a unique 'Navi-Key' touchpad system. He picked it up, and checked the screen, pleasantly surprised to see the name 'Harry' come up there.

'Sorry, folks, I gotta take this call.' He flashed them a look of apology, and turned back to the phone. "Harry! ... What's happening?'

At the mention of the name, Peaches stopped sauntering by the pool, and turned to look at Hyman. His dressing gown had fallen open to reveal his considerable paunch, white like the belly of the whale, and mottled with the same fine dark hairs that covered the rest of his body. But it was his demeanour she noticed. The sudden change in his tone, from frivolous to highly attentive.

'I haven't seen anything,' Harry said into the phone. 'No, I'm sitting down by the pool with a couple of friends ... We thought maybe you might like to come over ...' Hyman scratched his belly, gazing out over the ocean. Peaches observed him, her senses trained to nuance. She sensed something had happened, but had no idea what it might be. '... OK, sure, Harry. I'll call you back.' Hyman ended the call, and stood, mystified.

'What's up?' Peaches said.

'I've gotta go up to the house, check something out. Relax. I'll be back soon.'

They watched Hyman make his way up the steps to the portico, probably the only exercise he got, apart from the treadmill he had in his basement that he used occasionally.

Rosa came to the door, her expression difficult to interpret from the poolside. They watched Hyman go inside. Rosa shut the door behind him.

'What was that all about?' Dino said.

'Who knows? He was talking to Harry. It sounded a bit … ominous.'

Hyman's colonial style villa took on a brooding, melancholic character, with its fringe of tall palm trees and neatly-tended borders. The exotic flowers and brilliant gold of the bougainvillea created a rich palette for visitors to admire. Even the young actors on this particular stage, who weren't usually struck with such things, could appreciate the aesthetic. But now there was a different mood in the camp. Something was up, and they just had to wait around to find out what it was.

Peaches gazed up at the house, where the door had closed behind the imposing figure of Hyman. She had a feeling, a kind of foreboding. But when she looked to Dino to share her concern, he was lounging in Hyman's chair with Hyman's sunglasses on, as if he'd just usurped the man's position.

'What're you doing?' she said.

'Just wondering what it'd be like to be Hyman.'

'Take them off, it's disrespectful.'

'Since when did you care about stuff like that?'

'Just take them off!'

'Fuck's the matter with you?' He stared at her, defiant, immovable. 'Take it easy, for Christ sake.'

Her thoughts drifted, trancelike in the heat. Sometimes Dino made her so mad she could easily lose him, or go fuck someone else insted. She saw herself riding with the Sheik in his convertible, newly-installed as his favourite, having beaten off the competition. As his 'girl', she would have unlimited access to his charge account, and all the boutiques and department stores on Sunset Boulevard would welcome her like royalty. The Sheik wasn't really a sheik, of course, but a shady Moroccan drug dealer with a silver tongue and a big cock. He'd fooled a lot of people – including Hyman for a short while. Peaches had met him once in a night club on the Strip, and ended up going back to his apartment at Laguna Beach, primarily because he talked her into it and she'd been too drunk to say no. The first time she'd seen Dino throw a major tantrum, yelling at her for failing to come home, and making him think she'd been raped and murdered or something. The truth was, she had a great time and didn't regret any of it.

The Sheik was one of those rare men, as elusive as *she* was, with a hint of danger thrown in. When she was with him he made her feel alive, the sense that anything could happen. Dino was too possessive, but she loved him too much to break it off between them. They just needed a little time apart now and then.

'Maybe I should go up to the house,' she said. 'See what's going on.'

'Ask Hyman about lunch while you're up there. I haven't eaten since eight o'clock this morning.'

She hesitated, still fazed by Hyman's brief phone call with Harry. Then Rosa's synchronised appearance in the doorway as he got to the top of the steps. She couldn't help feeling resentful whatever it was. Today, on her birthday of all days, when she had plans to celebrate and have a good time.

'I was hoping we could've met Harry,' she said. 'He was going to introduce me to someone at Paramount Studios.'

'To do what?'

She fired him a scornful look. 'I don't know why I tell you anything sometimes. You're such a downer on everything I try to do.'

'Jesus. I didn't say anything?'

'You didn't have to. I can tell what you're thinking.'

Hyman reappeared, and wandered down from the house. He walked with his head down, solemn and contemplative, his beloved Nokia in his hand.

'He's coming back,' Peaches said. 'Get out of his chair ... and take those fucking sunglasses off, *please*!'

Reluctantly, Dino complied, vacating the chair to resume his place back at the table. They watched Hyman make his way down the steps, noting how gingerly he placed each footfall. His sluggish passage across the lawn and brooding air confirmed Peaches' fears. Something bad must've happened.

Hyman slumped into his chair, and stared at the pool. He had a glassy, unseeing look that seemed to block everything else out.

'Is everything OK?' Peaches said.

The air around them seemed to thicken. Hyman's breath came in shallow starts, his mouth open in a parody of disbelief.

'Someone shot him.'

'Who – Harry?'

Hyman turned to Peaches with a pained expression.

'Gianni ... This morning, outside his house.'

Peaches tried to grasp the significance, convinced she must've got it wrong.

'You don't mean? ...'

Hyman nodded, still dazed. 'I can't believe it ... On the steps of his fucking house as well.'

Peaches tried to find the words but none came. She knew who Hyman was talking about, but couldn't bring herself to have it confirmed. Instead, she recalled Gianni's mansion at Miami Beach, and the times she'd been there as a guest. It sounded inconceivable that someone who'd featured so prominently in her life could be a victim of something as awful as that.

'Was it fatal?' Dino said.

'Some fucking maniac just walked up and shot him twice at point blank range.'

Overcome by the awful finality, Peaches burst into tears. The mood of the day changed inexorably. The body-hugging red dress Hyman had laid out on the bed for her to find, took on an unfortunate symbolism. She wanted to take it off, and put her old clothes back on, distance herself from what had happened.

'Do you want us to go?' she said, drying her eyes.

Hyman looked up, bewildered. 'No, of course not. I'm just in shock, I guess.'

He called up Rosa on his Nokia, and asked for more drinks; the dutiful Mexican housekeeper, whose role was to look after Hyman and entertain his friends. Now she would be the one to console him, bringing refreshments for the recently bereaved.

The spectre of Versace's death hung over them as they sat by the pool. Something they couldn't escape. Peaches recognised the need to discuss it in some way, to give Hyman the opportunity to express how he felt, and to give her some kind of an explanation.

'Have they caught whoever did it?' she said.

'They're saying it was some young guy with a grudge against him. They've launched a manhunt all over Florida.'

'Did Gianni have any enemies?' Dino said.

'He was famous and he had money. What more do you need?' Hyman stared into the pool as if it contained the answer. 'What kind of a sick world are we living in? No one's safe anymore.'

Peaches looked up to the house with its arched portico and long balcony, the fringe of tall palms behind and above it. Versace's death put a different spin on things. Somehow, the privileged life they'd taken for granted had been exposed and threatened by an outsider. She didn't want to think there were people like that in her world, who were disturbed enough to kill just to make a point. Maybe there was someone out there obsessed enough to shoot *her* at point blank range; she could almost hear the fatal gunshot, see the headlines carrying the news of her demise.

Rosa brought the drinks down, and set them on the table. Peaches sank into a chair, and stared at the ice bobbing in the tall glass. The thought struck her that Gianni would never see the sunrise again, or the light sparkling on the surface of the water. Then, without prompting, another thought that his death had come at the most inconvenient time. How could she possibly celebrate her birthday now, knowing what had happened?

'That's it, then,' she said softly. 'I feel like the world just ended.'

Dino kept quiet. He had his own views and didn't particularly want to say how he felt. The Versace thing spooked him, but perhaps not in the same way. All the girls he knew in the industry had a special bond with the designers, and Peaches was no exception. His ongoing concern was still his relationship with her, and the uncertainty surrounding it. Like Hyman's house that sat atop the rise, she was his own piece of quality real estate, one that never failed to arouse a sense of ownership and the worries that went with it. Whenever he looked at her he was reminded of his good fortune. The body perfect, the coppertone skin. The hours of coke-fuelled sex that sometimes resulted in his inability to finish – a factor that sent Peaches into paroxysms of rage and humiliation.

Lately, the life they lived seemed empty of substance, like a hollowed out tube. They drifted from one day to the next in a haze of ever-diminishing expectations. The people they knew were trapped in a similar vacuum, existing on the periphery like extras in a movie. The shooting in Miami seemed to symbolise that lifestyle in some way, like a warning from the universe. Versace had been a star in his own right, having made the girls who modelled his creations into household names. Christy Turlington. Naomi Campbell. Cindy Crawford. The girls all loved him and treated him like a god. It seemed inconceivable that someone would want to kill him.

'I gotta call Harry back,' Hyman said, grabbing his Nokia from the table. He tapped in the number, and held the device to his ear, staring again into the pool, the surface still as a sheet of glass. When the call connected, he turned away, lowering his voice in an attempt at privacy.

Dino wandered over to the end of the pool to give Hyman some space. Peaches joined him.

'What's up?' she said.

'Nothing. Just getting out of Hyman's way.'

'Maybe we should go. I can't stand this horrible atmosphere.'

'What about your birthday? The celebrations?'

'After what happened to Gianni?' She gazed off at the heat haze that rose from the valley below. 'Whatever you had planned for me you'd better cancel. This is just about the biggest downer anyone could think of.' She started to cry again, her shoulders rocking to a plaintive rhythm. Dino reached out instinctively and held her in his embrace.

Hyman finished the call, and sat in silence on the edge of his chair. Peaches and Dino stood by the pool, their backs to him, their conversation muted and indistinct, somehow excluding him. Seeing them together inspired a feeling of tenderness and responsibility deep within him. Peaches' red dress took on a poignant significance. Had he known what was going to happen, he would've thought of something else to give to her. Now, in the light of Versace's death, it'd become an omen of some sort, an exotic focal point his eye kept returning to over and over.

'Harry's gonna join us,' he said finally.

They turned in unison, Peaches with a look of surprise.

'What – now?'

'It's a thirty-minute drive from the other side of town. Stay if you like, I've got no problem with you being here. In fact, I could use the company.'

Peaches tried to hide her relief, but Dino saw through it. This obsession she had to meet Harry, and the lengths she'd gone to in order to initiate it. Knowing Hyman was one thing, but an introduction to someone like Harry was another. He moved in a different world, one that Dino was unsure of. There were stories about him, linking him to a side of LA most people didn't get to hear about.

'Maybe we *should* go,' he said, echoing Peaches' earlier thought. 'It's a long drive back, and I've got calls to make, people to contact.'

'I don't want to.' Peaches stared hard at him, a wild and desperate look in her eyes. 'I think we should stay here and be with Hyman, he's obviously still shaken up – aren't you, Hyman?'

Hyman smiled sadly at her, his gaze misting over. 'Thanks, sweetie. But you do what you gotta do. Don't worry about me, I'll be fine.'

After further discussion, Peaches and Dino decided to stay. Hyman poured the drinks, and the three of them resumed their vigil at the ornate table beneath the umbrella. The occasionally tense dynamics between his two guests didn't concern him too much. Having recently recovered from a particularly troublesome love affair, he'd relearnt the art of self-sufficiency – albeit with the help of Rosa, and a local male escort agency which understood the concept of discretion and was rewarded handsomely for it.

Hyman liked to think that he'd lived his life to the full, having had many lovers, and many nights of such hedonistic pleasure that they blurred in his memory when he tried to recall them individually. The gay lifestyle had come at a time when he was just finding his feet in New York. Swept up in the rampant euphoria of Fire Island, and the heaving, adrenalin-charged nights in the Meatpacking District and Hell's Kitchen, he found the brotherhood which would embrace and haunt him for the next ten years.

Now Versace, cut down outside his home for no apparent reason by a madman with a gun. The thought sent a chill of dread through him, playing upon his lifelong fear of death. Looking up at his own lavish home sat atop the rise, it was hard to believe that one day it might belong to someone else. That Hyman would be no more than a brief obituary in the local paper, noting his achievements and next of kin. A spectacular send-off mentioned in the trade papers, then nothing. Obscurity.

Looking at Peaches, he felt a wave of paternal affection. He didn't envy her youth, or her seeming ability to process bad news as if it was a minor inconvenience. But he felt for her, even loved her in his own way, as a teacher feels love for a star pupil who has all the potential in the world but lacks guidance. She had her own journey to make, and he wished her well. But tonight he needed hers and Dino's company more than ever. He didn't want to be alone with Harry, whose cynicism and bad jokes could be draining; this private admission made him feel even wearier. Hyman the impresario, the extravagant host who brought people together with a mixture of his considerable charm and the promise of his good connections. People remembered his parties years later. Versace's death put it all into perspective. The gloom it cast seemed to have paled even the California sunshine, like someone had thrown the switch in a brightly-lit room.

The stirrings of some long forgotten impulse fought its way through. Peaches in the red dress. Dino beside her with his movie star looks. Some of Hyman's indomitable spirit returned, his refusal to be cowed by adverse circumstances.

'You know what I think you kids should do?' he said. 'I think you should jump on a plane to Vegas and get married.'

Peaches gawped at him.

'Seriously?'

'Why not? That's what's missing these days. The spirit of romance.'

Peaches looked Dino up and down, as if seeing him in a new light. 'We wouldn't last five minutes,' she said. 'He's too lazy, for a start. And I wasn't put on this earth to pick someone's clothes up off the bedroom floor.'

And so the mood changed, from sombre reflection to a hesitant optimism. The bad news became a catalyst, prompting a rebellion of sorts, and for Peaches in particular, a welcome return to form.

Hyman took a sip of his cocktail, and looked at Dino. 'What do you think?'

Dino understood right away. He gazed out at the coastline far below, weighing up the options.

'I think we should go ahead.'

Peaches also understood, that this wasn't just about her, but about a stand they were taking against bad luck and bad people.

They stayed by the pool all afternoon and into the evening, until the Californian light began to fade over the valley. Hyman had Rosa bring food down, and they all ate around a table overcrowded with bottles of wine and the spirit of companionship that came at the end of a long and traumatic day. Harry didn't turn up after all, on account of his plans changing at the last minute, a turn out Hyman was quietly grateful for, in spite of Peaches' initial disappointment.

They drank to Versace, whose spirit looked down on them from a far-off place. And Hyman gave thanks for present company. Dino with his understated humour and dark good looks. And Peaches, in her body-hugging red dress.

Later, against the prevailing mood, they celebrated Peaches' 21st at Hyman's Roman villa. The garden swelled with guests, the whole thing planned and organised by Dino weeks beforehand. Peaches shone like the star that she was, surrounded by the lights, the iridescent blue of the pool, and the beautiful people. And life went on as it always had done, turning night into day, and friends into lovers. And if Gianni Versace really had been looking down, he might've smiled in appreciation, with the feeling that it had all ended well. The life force that's in everyone, that shines like the sun, casting its glow upon each generation.

Zero-Sum Game

Airport waiting lounges are strange places. There's a palpable air of inertia, even though the entire concept is built on transience and movement. The human cargo sit around in varying states of lethargy and boredom, their mood offset by the imminent prospect of travel somewhere up ahead. There's the seasoned commuter, whose status reflects a certain stoicism. He sits alone, newspaper in hand, reading an article on the Polar icecap and its impact on the environment; the report worries him, but in a vague, disconnected way; his own issues seem to have more immediacy, playing on his mind and keeping him awake at night.

The two kids running up and down in the next aisle start to bother him. The disturbance sets off the nerve in his cheek that clicks like a metronome, distracting him from the words on the page. A large, heavy-set fellow, he carries his extra pounds well, his general demeanour reminiscent of the tough guys he grew up with on the streets of New York. He has a wife and child at home, and misses them intensely, often spending several weeks travelling for the engineering company he works for; the brownstone they live in in Boston's Back Bay area is always on his mind. But he's focussed on the trip ahead, and the opportunities it might offer in terms of their future wellbeing.

The parents of the two kids running up and down the aisle sit together but somehow apart, such is the level of their insularity. The husband is of average build, athletic looking, with a lean face and cropped military style hair. He carries himself with a soldier's confident bearing, used to a life of discipline and physical fitness in the Marine Corps. Irritated by the kids' performance, he can't be bothered to tell them again, leaving it to his wife to maintain the discipline. To counter the tedium, he observes the woman sitting across the way, who was standing in front of them when they checked-in. She seemed flustered, irritated by the security questions put to her by the ground crew.

'Has anyone unknown to you, asked you to carry an item on-board the aircraft for them?'

'No.'

'Have any of your bags been out of your sight since you packed them?'

'No.'

'Do you have any baggage to check?'

'No, I don't. Can I go now?'

The husband remembers her setting off the alarm when she went through the metal detector, and how embarrassed she looked, hurrying off with her bag over her shoulder. He pictures the two of them alone in a hotel room, fooling around on the bed. What he doesn't know is that the woman is a flight attendant, currently taking one of her staff travel concessionary flights to LA to stay with her sister. She hasn't had a relationship with a man since she split with her boyfriend, and is content being single.

His idle sexual fantasy is interrupted by his little girl, who trips, and lands face down on the terminal floor with a resounding 'slap!' She starts to cry, but in a reflex way, the sound soon lost in the vastness of the interior. He picks her up, and comforts her, kissing her tear-stained cheek. Soon they'll be on the plane, he tells her. She'll be able to get something to eat, maybe watch a movie.

His wife grabs the boy by the wrist as he runs past, and yanks him towards her.

'How many times do I have to tell you!' she snaps. 'Do you want me to take you home? Is that what you want?'

The boy slumps back onto the seat beside her, his freedom curtailed for the moment. His sister joins him, and they sit in silent protest, sharing the indignity of being children, pulled into line by parents who've long since abandoned the flights of imagination that enable them to escape the mundane. The children understand this on a deep, subconscious level , but it doesn't make it any easier. Adults are like the teachers at school, whose main job is to yell at them and stop them having a good time.

The flight attendant reads a magazine, unwittingly drawn in to the lives of her fellow passengers. She noticed the husband staring at her earlier. Apart from the fact he's not her type, they're not even in the same social bracket, and probably wouldn't have much in common anyway. As a flight attendant she's used to dealing with all kinds of people, and can often pick out the potential troublemakers as soon as they board the plane. This time she's a passenger herself, looking forward to the short break in LA. But she can't help a routine assessment of all the new arrivals out of habit.

She catches the husband staring at her again. He quickly looks away and assumes an air of disinterest; leaning back, he puts his hands behind his head and crosses his legs in an overtly male kind of way. His stance unsettles her in a way she doesn't really understand; it happens automatically, an unconscious impulse that occurs in a millisecond, before she's even aware of it. The great computer that runs her complex system, decides on her likes and dislikes from the storehouse of information that's fed in on a daily basis; from the slice of walnut cake she ate in the coffee shop earlier, to the pilot she saw strolling through Arrivals.

The pilot does something for her on a basic primal level she has no control over. To her he represents authority, glamour and excitement. By the time she gets to Passport Control she's almost forgotten him, her thoughts consumed by the prospect of the journey ahead. But he's there somewhere in the background, a powerful symbol that beckons to her from some hazy periphery.

Like the seasoned commuter, travel represents both a means of making a living *and* a way of life. This time, however, she's flying alone and out of uniform. The recent split with her boyfriend is the catalyst, from the shock of being abandoned for someone else, to a feeling of resilience. Now she can take charge of her life and do whatever she likes. She wears her newfound determination like a medallion that wards off evil – *and* the potential advances of men she has no interest in. Over time, this bitterness she feels towards men in general has eased; the glimpse of the airline pilot and the emotional jolt she receives from his image proves this unequivocally. But she remains cautious, aware of the personal upheaval any future liaison would bring.

Like everyone else in the airport terminal she's susceptible to a deeper and more mysterious level of awareness. She has no control over the thoughts that pop into her head or the feelings initiated by them. The rational, discerning part of her brain will always succumb to the powerful vat of chemicals that bubble beneath the surface.

A Hispanic looking guy drops into a seat near hers. He's dressed in jeans and a faded brown leather jacket that has zipped pockets. She's instantly defensive, conscious that he's invaded her space somehow. He gives her a token smile, and she smiles back, knowing that at some point he's going to make conversation, to establish some kind of connection between them as they wait for their flights.

Sure enough, like a scene from a movie, he makes his move.

'Excuse me?' he says.

She looks up in anticipation. He has a pleasant, inoffensive look on his face that's instantly disarming.

'Are you on the 8 o'clock to LA?' he says.

'I am, yes.'

He nods agreeably. 'I hope it's not delayed. I'm starting a new job, so I'd like to make a good impression.'

He tells her he's a computer programmer, and up until recently was living with his parents in Boston. Now it's time to move on, and venture out into the world to make his own way. He talks in a quiet, self-deprecating kind of way, that enables her to respond. She tells him about her background, her job with the airline, and gradually warms to him, without feeling put upon in any way. He seems like a regular guy just making conversation. They discover they have a shared love of *Friends*, and she tells him she's seen every episode. He says he loves the one when Chandler is smitten with Monica's roommate and can barely speak. The clock ticks down the time until they can board the plane. Neither of them has any idea of what lies ahead, or how the small details of their lives will take on a profound significance.

The seasoned commuter turns the page of his newspaper, glancing over the text without really taking it in. The small lump in his groin he discovered recently has grown in his imagination to become a cancerous tumour, which will undoubtedly be the cause of his early demise. He doesn't know that the lump is a benign cyst, removable through a minor operation, but its presence is enough to disturb his equilibrium and cause him to suffer unduly.

To offset these dark thoughts, he plans his funeral, picturing friends and family, who stand at his graveside weeping. This vision gives him a strange comfort, enabling him to go on with the business of living while he still has time. When he returns from his trip he'll make an appointment to see the doctor, an event his mind processes as being far enough ahead in the future not to worry too much about. Worry is a cancer in itself, that eats away at all the good things in life. He's generally upbeat and positive, making the most of whatever comes his way.

The harassed wife sits alongside her children, who behave like prisoners under duress. To them, the airport lounge is a vast playground to be explored whenever possible. Commuters pass by dragging their suitcases, an exodus from the mundane world they've all come from. The boy kicks his heels against the metal rim of his seat and thinks about *Space Bandits*, his favourite comic. He loves the bit when Captain Garcia destroys the aliens with his laser gun, averting disaster for the ship and the crew. Not yet consumed by the demands of adulthood, the boy sees the comic book spectacles on the cinema screen of his mind, his cerebral cortex lighting up with each viewing.

His sister sits with her father, who soothes her with kind words, and promises of all the things they'll do when they reach their destination. She clutches the rag doll she takes everywhere with her, and talks to in a voice she borrowed partly from her mother. Already, she's learned the uneasy balance of power that exists between her parents, and how to manipulate it to her advantage. Her father is often away with the Marine Corps, leaving her mother to oversee the children's behaviour and enforce discipline. Her mother cries a lot, sometimes without apparent reason, but they all have to get along together when he's away, so she does her best not to antagonise the situation. The little girl is largely unaware of these observations that go on beneath the level of her consciousness. All she knows is that life is sometimes unfair, and that she often gets the blame for things she hasn't done.

New arrivals cause a general speculation among the passengers. Two nuns wearing the traditional black habit and white headdress. The sisters park their hand luggage, and take a seat, seemingly oblivious to the interest of their fellow travellers. There's a lively animation about them, a shared humour reflected in their plump faces and twinkling eyes. If ever there was an advert for the benefits of religion this would seem to be it.

The harassed wife overhears the nuns talking, or at least a sense of their conversation that drifts over from where they're sitting – in between announcements over the Tannoy and complaints from her daughter, who's bored and hungry, two of the most problematic conditions a child can have. She strains to hear the nuns' topic of interest, amazed to realise they're actually discussing the marriage of a celebrity that's been in the news recently. What's more, they seem to be sharing bits of gossip, as if the celebrity in question is known to them personally. This strikes the wife as incongruous. Surely, they should be discussing matters of a religious nature in keeping with their vocation? And yet, their enthusiastic chatter does have an infectious ring to it, the two of them painting a strange picture in a place as bland and prosaic as an airport terminal.

The flight attendant observes the nuns from her seat a little further along. She's intrigued by their general demeanour, at odds with the early morning business types that populate the seating area. She recalls a nun she once served on a flight to Hawaii, who said she was competing in an Ironman triathlon; the woman said she'd taken up sport in her late 40s on the recommendation of a priest, who told her that running brought you closer to God. It seems inconceivable that a nun of all people would even contemplate taking part in such an extreme event, but stranger things happen.

Everyone, it seems, was searching for a higher purpose, a way to transcend the human frailties that made life so difficult at times. Divorced by the age of 28, and in debt to the tune of $40,000, the flight attendant can claim no such special dispensation herself. *To be human is to suffer* – a line she read somewhere that seems to ring true. And yet some people seemed to suffer more than others. Perhaps the nuns had found a way of dealing with this apparent injustice without it affecting their beliefs.

The Hispanic looking guy takes some papers from his case, and looks through them. She senses a quiet reticence in him; since their initial conversation he's retreated, absorbed in his own space. They're strangers again, with nothing in common but the flight they're soon to be taking. And yet she feels compelled to speak to him, to pick up the thread they established earlier.

'You must be looking forward to your new job?' she says.

He looks up and smiles. 'I was actually thinking of getting a job here at the airport. A friend of mine works here as an air traffic controller. Pays good, and there's great discount for employees.'

He has nice eyes, warm and tinged with humour. Maybe under different circumstances she might've responded and opened up a bit more. Just not here in the airport terminal. Her head's not in the right place.

The seasoned commuter also notes the nuns arrival. Unlike the flight attendant, their presence arouses in him a feeling of ambivalence. They appear almost childlike in their chatter, a kind of innocence about them that belies the solemn nature of their vocation. The nuns he remembers from his schooldays were stern and unforgiving, capable of dishing out physical punishment for the slightest infraction. He sees the classroom with its rows of wooden desks, pitted and scarred from the countless incumbents who'd been there before him. And yet, aspects of that time had been pleasurable. The friends he'd made there, some of whom he still sees to this day, who came from the same impoverished and abusive backgrounds. They formed little cliques, quietly rebelling against the authority imposed upon them, enjoying the camaraderie that drew them closer together. These things he recalls with a keen nostalgia, like the family he hasn't seen much of recently because of his schedule. He plans to ease up on the travelling, maybe take a job closer to home so he can spend more time with his wife and kids.

The little girl sits quietly. She clutches her ragdoll and talks to it in soothing tones. 'Soon we'll be on the plane,' she whispers, 'and the horrible person won't be able to keep on at us anymore.' Glancing over at her mother, she reminds the doll that it won't be long now, reminding her how exciting it'll be to fly to another state. She's never been to LA before, and looks forward to staying with her grandmother, who lives in a place called Redondo Beach. She loves her grandmother very much, especially as she never shouts or gets angry. She loves her mother too, but just not in the same way.

Her brother eats the candy bar his mother gave him to keep him quiet, and thinks about killing aliens with a laser gun. In the last issue of *Space Bandits*, Captain Garcia steers the ship into the forbidden galaxy and challenges the leader of the alien spacecraft to a duel. The boy's fantasies of spaceflight and derring-do are interrupted by the sound of his sister's hushed voice talking to the ragdoll. She loves the doll more than anything else, and plays with it for hours on end, carrying it round with her wherever she goes.

The sight inspires in him a mischievous urge. Reaching over, he snatches it from her, anticipating her stricken reaction and the punishment he'll face from their mother. Holding the doll up out of his sister's reach, he fends off the retaliation, even as his mother pitches in to wrestle it from his grasp. She looms over him, red-faced and teeth clenched, like one of the aliens faced by Captain

Garcia. 'What's the matter with you!' she says, in her angry mom's voice. 'How many times do I have to tell you! You want me to take you home? Is that what you want?'

The husband intervenes, ordering the boy to sit with him, away from the little girl, whose successful retrieval of the doll has pacified her somewhat. Mission accomplished, the boy sits back and hums to himself, kicking his heel against the metal strut of the seat. He's unaware of the trials that await him up ahead, where the cartoon world of spaceships and laser guns will take on a terrifying lifelike quality.

The flight attendant witnesses the altercation, her decision not to have children vindicated. She identifies, even empathises with the mother, whose frustration is still evident in her red face. Naturally, questions arise. Why do people allow their kids to misbehave in public places? Surely, it's a reflection of their failure as parents?

She turns the pages of her magazine; something satisfying about the feel of the glossy paper between her fingers, and the bright colour photographs that reflect the overhead light. The models in the adverts are all very young, wearing clothes more suited to an older generation. It makes them appear more ordinary, almost asexual somehow, with their long, floral dresses and knitted cardigans. She can't imagine them in short skirts and heels, animated with a boundless energy like some of her friends.

The clock ticks for her also. Unlike the boy sitting with his father, whose concept of time is measured in long chunks of boredom offset by the TV, hers is anchored firmly in the here and now. When she looks in the mirror, she sees a plain and unresponsive face, that seems to accentuate the disenchantment she sometimes feels. But her self-conscious fears are largely unwarranted. Most men find her attractive; she draws admiring glances from strangers, and is a popular member of every crew she gets to work with.

Her job as a flight attendant means she has to be 'on' most of the time. Everything has to be just right, from the uniform and the choice of footwear, to the tone of voice she uses to talk to passengers on-board each flight. Sometimes she can't help feeling responsible for everything, as if its hardwired into her DNA. But the job satisfies something deeper in her, the need to take care of people, to make sure they're comfortable and have everything they want for the duration of the flight. She gets a feeling of satisfaction whenever they land, and she sees them all safely off the plane.

The affair she once had with a pilot pops up in her head. She pictures them at the exotic resort in Mauritius they stayed at, sitting at an outdoor table overlooking the sea. Then later in the hotel room, where the windows opened onto a moonlit terrace. Even here in the airport lounge surrounded by people, she feels the accompanying rush of chemicals that brings life to the scene.

When she looks up, she's surprised to see that the nuns have gone, their seats conspicuously vacant. Late arrivals file in, dressed in open-necked shirts and hats, reflecting the unusually warm September weather. They gaze up at the ticker boards in expectation, fellow travellers, all sharing this journey with its long periods of boredom, sitting around with nothing to do.

The seasoned commuter discards his paper in favour of a stretch. His plane is due to leave on the hour, and already he's jittery – a familiar pre-flight nervousness he's had ever since he can remember. He thinks about ordering a drink on the plane, a reasonable enough idea even at that time in the morning, except that the one would inevitably lead to another – the same crash he'd get eventually from taking a pill. Instead, he decides to sit it out, recalling the theory of delayed gratification, instilled in him during his youth when he used to play college football. Physical ailments aside, he's done reasonably well to reach the age he's currently at, even if it is a non-negotiable number that keeps accumulating every year.

To offset the boredom, he amuses himself with different scenarios. The prospect of a plane crash appeals to his morbid sense of humour. Investigators would find his body parts strewn amongst the wreckage, along with the undiagnosed tumour, the cancerous growth and the varicose veins. This semi-humorous speculation helps him process something that's out of his control. But what he doesn't know, is that in less than an hour he'll encounter a situation he could never have prepared for. His entire life will unfold before him like the scenes from a movie.

The harassed wife focusses on the children, and the ceaseless job of keeping them amused. In many ways it would've been better if they'd stayed with her parents, but that would've put too much of a strain on them, as they're both getting on in years and don't have the same energy. The thought brings on a feeling of guilt. How bad was it to wish you were away from your own children? And yet sometimes they were exasperating, often to the point where she wanted to scream. The boy especially, with his sullenness and refusal to do as he's told.

Glancing at him across the seats, she sees his stoic look of acceptance, that can only mean he's plotting a way to get even later on. Her husband's equally to blame. Rather than reprimand the boy himself, supporting her and creating a unified front, he chooses to hold off, leaving it to her to sort out. The girl has her own way of getting round him, even down to the whining tone she uses, and the selective use of certain facial expressions to weaken his resolve. But that's just a long-running tape that plays in the background. She loves her children unconditionally, and tries not to take her frustrations out on them.

Much as she would never admit it to anyone else, she sometimes resents her husband, who's often away with the military. She suspects him of having affairs, but has never asked him outright. Years ago she met a man through the yoga class she was attending, and one thing led to another. They slept together a few times, something she came to regret. But whatever the obstacles that've come along, her marriage has held together. And in spite of his tendency to be an asshole now and then, she loves her husband and can't see herself with anyone else.

The boy has succumbed to the inertia; even his legs have stopped swinging. He chews his lower lip instead, staring up at the tubular struts of the ceiling. The configuration reminds him of a huge spaceship, one they're all on board, heading for a far-off galaxy.

His father bends to whisper something to him, a joke shared

between the two of them that deliberately excludes his mother and sister. The boy smiles, enjoying this momentary diversion and the air of complicity it creates between him and his father. He looks at his watch, and touches the hard, moulded edges with fascination. The device gives him a great deal of pleasure every time he looks at it; its face a complex pattern of numbers and symbols, like the one Captain Garcia wears that has special powers. He fantasises that his watch has similar capabilities, which he can activate at the touch of a button. He could use it on his mother every time she has a go at him, and make her disappear, transported into another dimension.

He watches the late arrivals, picking out the odd feature that amuses him in some way. They stare up at the ticker board, checking flight times and glancing at watches. The world he lives in is a perplexing mix of the real and the imaginary. To offset all the sitting around, he reverts to the fantasy in his head which is infinitely more interesting. In this realm, adults don't exist, except as peripheral figures who appear as extras, or simply remain in the background to be captured and rounded up – put on board vast spaceships that banish them to remote outer galaxies. Girls don't figure much either, falling into the same category as the adults. He tolerates them only because he has to. But like the seasoned commuter, and the rest of the passengers waiting to board the flight to LA, the boy has no idea of what lies ahead.

The husband counts down the time until they can board the plane. Out on the runway, one of the 767s is taxying, ready for take-off. It looks sleek and streamlined, its 'American' logo emblazoned on the side. He hopes they can board soon, especially for the boy's sake. Kids work on incentives, promises of treats up ahead. This seems to work better than the chastisements and random punishments dished out by his wife. She's always accusing him of being too lenient, which he thinks is unfair. She's changed a lot since they were married. These days it's hard to put a smile on her face; he can't remember the last time they went out on their own as a couple. Sex is a problem too. She's always too tired or too angry from dealing with the kids. But he wants to make it work and does what he can to make her happy. Maybe the family get-together at Thanksgiving will help bring them together. She gets on well with his mom and dad, and always says how close she feels to them. The previous year went well. It felt like they were a family again, the tensions of their marriage dissolved in a flow of harmony and good feeling.

The flight attendant watches them with interest. Something about the intimacy of the scene intrigues her, the way the father leans over to say something to the boy, and the boy's amused reaction. Her own father was remote, and often simply not there much of the time, always away on business, or whatever else he happened to be doing. The only gestures of affection she remembers were those prompted by her mother, simply to mark some calendar event he was obligated to attend, like a birthday or anniversary. And yet, she views him more favourably now – adulthood helping her unravel the confusion and make some sense of it all.

But like the seasoned commuter and the boy, she has no way of knowing how things will turn out. In less than an hour, she will leave her father a tearful message on her cell phone, saying how much she loves him and misses him, knowing that this will be the last communication they'll ever have.

'Would you like one of these?'

Looking up, she sees the Hispanic looking guy holding out a bag of sweets. She hesitates – accepting his offer might give him the wrong idea. But he's probably just being polite, so what the hell?

'Thanks,' she says, and takes one. The act has a kind of intimacy, a lowering of the barriers between them. She understands instinctively the need for communication, that it's a fundamental part of human nature. When she doesn't interact with other people she suffers.

Over the years she's tried many different ways of improving herself, including several years of therapy and the countless self-help books that fill her bookshelves at home. The relief these methods offer have been disappointing overall; although she has benefited from a heightened self-awareness and a new insight into the way she thinks. But underneath she still feels the same, a bit reserved and unsure around people. She wishes she could be more like her sister, who's outgoing and loves to socialise. They often joke that it's her sister who should be working on the airline, instead of her.

She once read a book that explained the nature of negative thoughts and their basic transience. It helped not to take them seriously sometimes, and to realise that everyone has them to a greater or lesser extent. But even after reading the book twice and practicing the suggestions, the thoughts were still there, like a rogue computer virus going over and over in her head.

The seasoned commuter shifts in the seat, and feels discreetly for the lump in his groin. It's there beneath his finger, an insinuation, larger in his imagination than it probably is in reality. He sits back and watches the latest arrivals, taking deep breaths to help calm down. Better to adopt the philosophical attitude instead. Plenty of people out there were going through worse things without making a fuss; the kid with leukaemia he read about, lying in a hospital bed with a big smile on his face, holding up a signed photograph of Lawrence Taylor.

Boarding opens for the passengers of Flight 175 to LA. There's a noticeable shift in the atmosphere, as the incumbents rouse themselves from their torpor in readiness for the next phase. The seasoned commuter checks his hand luggage, taking out his headset to use on the plane. Like everyone else, he's relieved that the waiting is over. People weren't designed for sitting around in a vacuum. Forward momentum is the governing agency in all human affairs. It feels good to be moving.

Two late arrivals show up, bags slung across their shoulders. They're male, Middle-Eastern looking. One wears steel-rimmed spectacles that give him a vague academic look. The other is nondescript, of college age. They look up at the ticker board for the latest flight information.

The flight attendant prepares herself for the coming journey. She sits up, and checks her watch. All across the terminal passengers prepare for embarkation. The husband and wife check their hand luggage and boarding passes, the wife taking it upon herself to be the chief organiser.

This mood of anticipation affects the boy and girl. They join their parents and other passengers in a queue for the exit that will take them out to the runway; the little girl clutches her ragdoll, and whispers to it as the queue moves forward. She's excited, perhaps that little bit more tolerant of her brother now, although she knows this won't last. But for now, theirs and everyone else's problems are relegated to the side-lines, in readiness for the coming flight – and in a sense, the unknown.

The two Middle-Eastern men check their boarding passes, and share a look of quiet resolve. Later, they're due to meet with colleagues on the same flight, to initiate the plans they've been moving steadily towards over the previous months. They have a different agenda to the other passengers, and are committed to seeing it through. In the luggage that's stored in the plane's hold, are documents relating to their goal. Quotations from religious texts urging them to be courageous and to pray for guidance from God. In carrying out their plans, they will make a profound statement that's seen by millions across the world, heralding a new era of fear and hostility.

The Captain strolls towards the Boeing 767 that sits on the runway awaiting his expertise. He's looking forward to the flight, and the destination at LA's central airport. The skies are blue and radiantly clear.

It's a perfect day in September.

A perfect day for flying.

FICTION

The Butterfly Collector

What happens when everything you have is not enough?

Restless property developer, Peter Calliet meets a sullen young woman at a party and an obsession begins that links past and present in a deepening tragedy.

Peter has everything in terms of material success and security. The obligatory fast car, lucrative contracts with his powerfully connected father's property empire and a plush renovated flat. Devoted fiancée, Claudia, expects to move in and marriage is imminent. But Peter has a dark past that taints his movements. Meeting Natalie, a volatile artist with an equally disturbed background, can only lead to more heartache. If Claudia discovers that Peter has been seeing Natalie, her dream world will be destroyed, adding to his burden of guilt. But even that can't stop him. The secure and rewarding life he has worked so hard to achieve begins to unravel.

'Peter Calliet is very believable, with that mix of liberal thinking and callousness that's essentially human.'
Nikki Copleston

'Dickson has a talent for expressing emotional anguish perfectly in prose and it makes the characters feel even more believable.'
The Kindle Book Review

FICTION

<u>Drowning by Numbers</u>

It's 1994. Blur and Oasis are in the charts. New Labour are on the horizon. Ladbroke Grove is the place, a thriving hub of art, music and cultural diversity.

Emerging from the wreckage of another lost weekend, Indie Guitarist of the Year, Joe E Byron, hurries home on the Tube to face the consequences of his actions. Ten years on the road has taken its toll. He should be spending more time with Justine and the kids. Instead, he's restless, angry, and in conflict with his manager and the rest of the band. Dark habits threaten his marriage and his career. The curse of addiction which will rob him of everything. And at the heart of it all, a yearning to be free, to take off and never come back.

But that can't happen.
There's too much at stake.
Besides,
He's a god.
He's a legend.
And the only thing worse than dying
is the prospect of fading away.

'If you're looking for a happy ever after ending, this book is probably not for you, but if you're looking for an excellent read with a hopeful ending, you will love Drowning by Numbers.'
Pamela Fudge

FICTION

<u>Billy Riley</u>

Fresh out of prison after five years, debt collector and one-time enforcer Billy Riley heads back to his council estate home with wife Eileen.

But things have changed since he's been away. The local kids run round in gangs, terrorising the neighbours with drive-by shootings and random drug deals. Respect for the old criminal hierarchy is gone. And turning 40 inside hasn't helped. His best years are behind him, future opportunities slipping away.

'Riveting... This begs to be adapted for the big screen!'
Jonathan Evans

'Hooked from the start, fascinating characters and a compelling storyline.'
EM Flattery

FICTION

<u>Indigo Blue</u>
California, 1939.

A glamorous young couple sail a yacht off the coast, heading for the Gulf of Mexico. Behind them, fragments of the turbulent life they've abandoned, recalled in flashbacks and poignant memories.

The actress, Laura-Mae, her promising career in Hollywood cut short in the most brutal of ways.

The opportunist, Johnny Boy, fleeing from the authorities with a headful of dreams.

Their love is of the special kind.
It protects and nurtures them,
inspires ambitious plans.
But there's a dark side too.
A threat to anyone who might uncover the truth.

NON-FICTION

<u>Surfing The Edge</u>
A Survivor's Guide To Bipolar Disorder

The TV's on
The computer's on
The stereo's on
Sleep is a waste of time

Welcome to the world of Bipolar Disorder, a journey to the outer edges of the mind. A series of conversations told with humour, honesty and insight by Adam, Faye and Alastair, three survivors who have experienced the illness first hand. With contributions from Mental Health professional, Chris Kelly.

'Couldn't put this down, it rang so many bells for me. I recommend this to sufferers and recoverers or even just the nosey parkers.'
Angela Warren

Ingram Content Group UK Ltd.
Milton Keynes UK
UKHW040127110723
424902UK00001B/10